Dawn of Hearts

Above the Ground Series

Nareena Rhoman

Copyright © 2024 Nareena Rhoman

All rights reserved

Contact: NareenaRhomanBooks@gmail.com

Map Illustration by Anna Dolidze
Contact: annanodolidze@gmail.com

Cover Illustration by Ozge Demir
Contact: demirozge1998@gmail.com

To my little sister, who is always bringing the magic out in me and making me believe anything is possible. Thank you for always bringing out my inner child and for keeping her alive…

And for all the girls who don't know what their place is in the world yet, but know that they were meant for something great. You will find it. Do not give up.

To the readers who wish that they could live between the pages of their books. To those who let stories consume them, enough so that it takes weeks to get over the heartbreak of finishing a book that you fell so in love with.

YRIA
The Fates
Kingdom of Darkness
the deserted human lands
Kingdom Of Light
the whisps
aging aborum

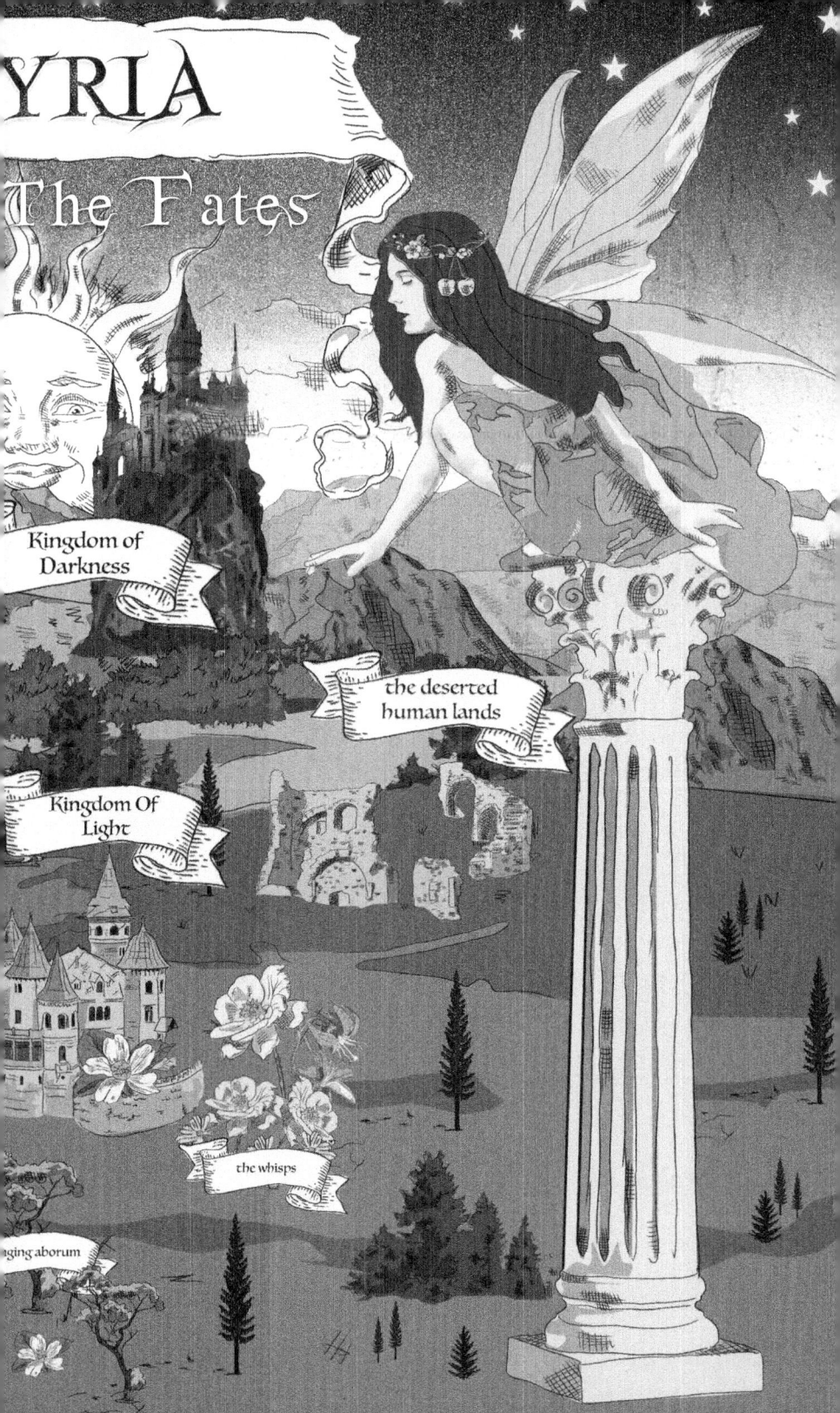

Prologue

"No more fairy tales. I don't know where you learned such things, but it ends now," the man screamed at the young woman.

"But there has to be something more—" the woman began.

"There is nothing MORE!" He pounded his fist on the table while interrupting her.

"I can't help but feel that way. That there is a piece of the world that I am missing." She sauntered towards her husband, wrapping her hand around his shaking arm.

"The only *piece* that you are missing is obeying your husband." He shook her off.

A single tear ran down her cheek as she rushed after him. "Is that all I am good for then? Obeying you?" she questioned, knowing that she could get into trouble for it, but she didn't care. She was so tired of pretending to be happy. Pretending like she could ignore the treatment of herself and the other women. She couldn't ignore it any longer, not like the others could.

He sighed as if she wasn't even worth the breath it took to give her an answer. "Of course that is all you are good for. It is *all* that your kind are good for," he said walking towards the front door.

Your kind.

As if women were a whole other species.

She wiped the wetness from her cheek, deciding that he wasn't worth her tears.

The young woman was also a mother.

She tucked her daughter into bed every night. Most nights, she whispered to her tales of hope, love, and magic. Ones that she had learned about in a book from long ago. A book that was forgotten and hidden in the library. When she first found it as a young child, she felt like it was hidden there especially for her.

For her and *only* her to find.

When she held that book in her hands and read the words written in it, it was like magic seeped out from the pages and flowed into her veins. It made her feel alive for the first time in her life.

It let her escape to a life that wasn't actually hers.

But that night, she felt like telling another story to her daughter. One of curses and true love. One that she she knew back to front, but couldn't quite place where she had read it.

She told the story, making sure to keep her voice down in case her husband had come back.

"Tell me the story again Mama!" the little girl begged. It was her bedtime, and her mother had already told her the same story twice.

"Shhhh, shhh…" the mother hushed her daughter. "My sweet rose, you must go to bed," She said as she pulled the blankets on the girl.

"Please, just one more time!" the girl begged.

"Fine. One more time, and then you are going to go to sleep."

"Deal!" The girl smiled wide with her two front teeth missing.

"Once upon a time, there was a land of magic… and two kingdoms ruled over the land: one of darkness, and one of light. There were people who lived in these kingdoms, and they too had magic. Everything was *perfect*."

"That's my favorite part," the girl whispered as she fought her tired eyes.

"Along with the people who possessed magic, there were those without it… humans," the mother said as she pinched the girl's cheek and smiled.

"The humans and the magical people lived side by side in harmony. They did not particularly *like* each other, but they were peaceful. Until one day, a human girl fell in love with a magical being from the land of darkness. They were so in love that they decided they were going to run away together, despite what their families wanted.

"The human girl ran from her home and made it all the way to the dark kingdom on foot before she saw that her true love had been killed. She was too late, and her fated match was dead. He was murdered by humans who heard of their love and did not approve of it, so they found a way to kill the immortal being. A poison that would truly end the immortal's life. It was because of their hatred that her true love had died.

"The human girl spent days, weeks, *months* in mourning. Some say that she cried for ten days straight when she found him, and there were enough tears to form a river through the woods that connected the humans to the land of darkness.

"Her love for him and the grief that she felt was so strong that it broke the peace between the peoples and the land fell apart. The thread of harmony that tied the magical beings and the humans together had snapped. It was as if a crack had been made in the world that could only be caused by true pain and loss and only healed by the opposite…*true love*.

"The death of her lover set in motion a spell on the lands… a *curse*. Through the soil of the cursed land sprouted another type of magical beings… ones not of human image. They were formed by the curse itself, from the despair and grief that consumed the human girl who had her heart broken. These creatures craved the one thing that they didn't have... *souls*. They scoured the land and searched for humans and magical beings alike to soak up their life source. The thing about these creatures, however, is that they never stop. They never get enough to satisfy, thus making it impossible for humans to dwell in the magical lands any longer.

"It is said that the only way for humans and magic to once again live side by side, is for a human girl to be matched by fate to one of these magical beings. If not, both humans and those who possess magic will surely come to an end. *What was broken must be mended.*"

"How will it fix if it is all up to fate? How will the girl know that it is up to her?" The young girl yawned as she finally gave into her heavy eyes.

"Everything is up to fate my dear. Everything happens the way it must." The mother gave a faint smile. "She won't have to know, the threads of fate will deem it so."

"How do you know this—?" The girl yawned again. "How do you know this story, Mama?" The girl thought about all the books in the library, and how she had never seen anything like the story her mother told, besides the few fairytale books hidden on the back shelf, untouched and covered in layers of dust. She figured that no one knew that they were even there.

The books told stories of kings and queens who fell in love and princesses who would only wake from their slumber with a true love's kiss. It felt as if those books had been placed there for *her*. As if she was *supposed* to find them. She had thought that the other books about war and different types of rocks were interesting until she found the storybooks. She then made it her mission to make sure no one else would ever find them, because if they did she knew that they would be taken from her.

The stories that made her dream and wish upon stars that she couldn't even see.

The mother thought for a moment as if she had never quite thought of the question herself. "I think that sometimes we are born with stories, things that we are just *supposed* to know. Things that are embedded into us and weaved into our very souls to be passed down. Some things, we just know without having to be told... and a magical story like this, it is quite possible that it is one that doesn't even need to be *told* for someone to know it."

"And now I know it!"

The mother smiled wide. "Yes, and now you know it." She brushed her hand upon the girl's cheek before she drifted to sleep.

The girl awoke in the middle of the night to raised voices sounding from down the hall.

"What did I tell you about the fairy tales?" her father's voice rang from the kitchen. Loud enough to scare the young girl, but not loud enough to wake up those who lived next to them. The girl lit the torch next to her bedside and crept towards her door. It was so dark she could barely make out anything, but enough to recognize the shapes of her mother and father's faces.

"She needs to have some sense of the world. She has to have hope, hope that there is something better—"

He charged toward the mother, and the girl gasped as he began to belittle her. He was saying things that would surely crack anyone's heart open, but the woman was strong.

It wasn't until his next words that the girl saw her mother with true fear in her eyes.

"If you ever fill her head with such nonsense again, I will turn you in. Tell them of all of the stories you have been feeding our daughter. You know what will happen to her then."

In that moment, she saw all the light that her mother had possessed extinguish into nothing but darkness.

The books that the girl had found hidden in the library disappeared the next day. She tried to remember the stories that she read as the weeks went by. She even tried to write them down along with the story her mother had told her. But as all stories do, without being read or told, they faded from her memory like dust in the wind.

PART ONE

The Underground

1

*Dread, impending doom, trepidation—*there were an infinite amount of words to describe what I was feeling, and none of them were what I *should* have felt.

I yanked the corset strings tighter around my waist as the few bites of food that I took at lunch started making their way back up. This day was supposed to be exciting. It was *supposed* to be the one day of my life that really mattered—the day that they prepared us for since birth.

"Us" as in the women.

Being the naive young girl that I was, as all young girls are, I imagined it to be the most *perfect* day.

It should start with a lavish breakfast and then hours and hours of getting ready. My long brown hair should flow gorgeously down my shoulders and I should be clothed in an elegant dress that complemented my body.

My only accurate prediction was the hours of getting ready. And that was *not* fun like I had dreamed it to be.

I had been a wishful child. Unpractical and too imaginative for my own good. I wasn't sure who I inherited that trait from, as it definitely wasn't from either of my parents.

Bland and cruel were the only words I could think of to describe them. I meant it as an insult, but the truth was it was what I wished I could be—the former, not the latter.

I grunted as I finished lacing up the bodice and turned sideways in the mirror to examine my squeezed-in waist. My reflection frowned back at me before I rushed over to grab my stockings from the nightstand.

My hands shook as I slid the thin tights up each of my legs. I wished that the day was already over before it even began.

For what was supposed to be *my* day, it sure felt like everyone else's. My mother chose the dress, the maids did my hair, and when it would come down to it, I wouldn't even get to choose who *he* would be.

I would be *chosen*.

Like a prized mare at an auction.

I didn't even know what that saying meant, but I learned it from one of the books from above. One of the few books left in the library from before.

Before the world was taken over by evil. None of us knew what happened exactly. It was over two hundred years ago, so we only knew what information was passed down from those who lived it.

But there was one fact that everybody knew. If we went up there, we die either from starvation and not knowing how to fend for one's self, or from the creatures that roam the land, hoping for a human to suck the soul out of. The latter was the most likely to happen.

For almost two hundred years, humans had lived underground, dwelling within the stone walls and the only light source being the torches and candles that we light. Our civilization is fairly large, even though it was made by digging tunnels through dirt and stone.

My mind snapped back to the task at hand as I finished rolling my stockings over my knees and up my thighs.

Not one part of that day was truly about me.

That harsh reality was what I came to realize as I grew older. I supposed that was why I quit dreaming of the perfect dress, the perfect hair, and the perfect companion.

Once, I mentioned my feelings to my mother and she called me ungrateful. I still remember that day, a little too clearly for my liking. I was thirteen years old.

I had asked her why women were taught to impress men, but men were not taught to impress women.

Why we were taught how to come off as confident, but not so much so that it would be mistaken for being promiscuous? Why we have to be elegant, but not boring? And funny, but not vulgar.

Why the women have to work so hard to be something else to please a man, but the men could just... *be*?

I asked her why women were taught to please the men if it was *our* special day.

Shouldn't they have been impressing us?

I never asked again.

Ungratefulness couldn't be further from the truth. It was actually quite a war I had with myself, constantly. I loved watching the matching ceremony every year, and I was happy for the girls who were happy to be chosen. But sometimes, I just wondered if there was another way. Or maybe I was just meant for something else.

Maybe it was the path for others, and mine was different.

Those feelings that I wrestled with weighed on me over the past few years. They whispered to me each time that I was made for more.

Not that I even knew what *more* was.

The helpers, and *maids*, of the underground were bustling around me. They were dressed in their usual loose clothing: a flowing beige top with a long beige skirt that stopped just above their ankles. Beige was the unofficial, but also official, designated color of the underground.

I always thought it was the easiest color to make everything, but now I was convinced that it was some sort of mind trick to keep us from wanting more. Being surrounded by the most boring color day and night never let us get a taste of what else there was. We would stay content.

Even though I knew that if anyone heard my thoughts, I would surely risk banishment, I couldn't stop. But that was why they stayed as thoughts. My mother had scolded me never to bring such things up again, and I knew it was for our safety.

If anyone truly knew what was going on in my head, I would be thrown to the wretched creatures above and never to be spoken of again. My family would be banished if they even mentioned my name afterward.

I tried to ignore the traitorous thoughts at first, but as time went on, they only became louder. Eventually, I let them flow freely because I realized no one else could hear them anyway. As long as they stayed in my head.

Although I had to admit, it was extremely hard at times. I didn't like not being able to tell Poppy how I truly felt. She was my best friend, and I felt like a liar for not telling her. Maybe she had those thoughts too?

Doubtful.

No one had those thoughts. Not one other person besides me. I wasn't sure why my mind worked the way it did. Why no one else dreamed of a different life? Why only my mind believed that there *could* be a different life.

The maids worked quickly, brushing out my dark brown, almost black, strands, before pulling them up into a tight high up-do, leaving two pieces out in the front to be braided.

Then, they started to apply rouge to my pale porcelain skin, adding some color to my face. The pinkish hues brightened my apple-shaped cheeks and added some life to my face that was not usually present. They slipped the beige silk dress that my mother picked out over the corset. It stopped just above my knee and the short sleeves were puffed out slightly.

As I glanced at the mirror, I wasn't quite sure who was looking back at me. A girl who I knew, but at the same time, one that I had never seen before.

Everything inside of me was pleading to myself to be proud of who I was and how I looked.

Not good enough.
"There is always room for improvement."

I recoiled at the words that repeated over and over in my head. The teachings and words that they had ingrained into our young minds haunted my perception of myself.

My eyes deflected from the illusion of my reflection as my mother called out to me. "Amara, staring at your reflection won't change anything. It is time for the ceremony," she said, and I could hear her footsteps leading towards the front door.

"Coming, Mother!" I called out as a tiny chunk of my heart fell to the floor at her words. I was used to her treatment, but that didn't mean it hurt any less.

When I passed the threshold, my body tensed as she examined me. Her eyes revealed nothing but a bored expression. Lifeless and empty.

"Good enough," she muttered as she held the front door open for me to pass through behind her.

"Thank you, Mother," I replied as I walked behind her with my hands folded into each other and my head down.

She huffed in response as if she hadn't meant her words as a compliment at all.

Our footsteps scuffed over the rough stone as we walked down the long hallway. It felt as if the walls were closing in on me, the hallway feeling tighter and tighter with each step that I took and the closer we came to the ceremony.

I tried to focus on anything but the nerves coursing through my body. I thought of the tunnels and how hard it must have been for the humans who had to dig them.

Apparently, it took the humans a whole twenty years to build the underground and get it to the point of being an actual village. It started as just a large hole underground to hide from the creatures of magic, and over time it morphed into an entire civilization. There were halls for events, a spot right in the middle where people gathered to talk or eat meals together, and hallways on each end of the underground where the living quarters were. The hallways split off into each dwelling with a front door separating families from each other.

Every room and area in the underground was built from the same cream-colored stone. It lined every surface and although some rooms were grand in size, they still looked the same as every other room.

The stone that I saw day and night made up every wall and every floor. I was so sick and tired of seeing that stone, but in that long walk that led me to my inevitable doom, I was thankful for the stone.

To drown myself in it and count the cracks as if counting them would take me away from where I really was. For a moment it worked until my mother came to an abrupt stop and I nearly ran into her.

We were there.

"I can't do this, Poppy," I said as I paced back and forth in the waiting room reserved for the women eligible for the matching.

"Yes, you can, Amara," she said, gripping onto my shoulders.

"No, I really can't." I wiped the beads of sweat from my forehead.

"You can… and you will." She shook me to force my eyes toward hers. "You're just nervous! It happens to everyone." She winked.

"Not you." I grimaced. "Not when you know Sam is going to pick you. You have your future planned out. Mine is… unknown."

She frowned. "I don't *know* for certain that he will pick me." She dropped her arms from my shoulders. "He could pick you." She laughed and punched my shoulder.

My face curled into disgust and she laughed even harder. "That would truly be the end of my existence," I joked. "No, but, seriously… Sam *loves* you. You two have loved each other since we were little children. You have nothing to worry about."

"I hope so." She turned and tapped her finger on her arm. Her golden hair swayed as she turned to face the mirror. She adjusted her gown that loosened at the hips and flowed past her ankles. She then stepped closer to get a better look at her face. Even in that dimly lit room, the reflection of the blue in her eyes sparkled and her smooth skin glistened.

We had been friends since childhood. Poppy and I. Sam was our friend too, but he was always extremely shy. However, since that was his only shortcoming, he was practically gold compared to the other men.

He and Poppy had denied feelings for each other since the moment they were introduced. I always saw the way he looked at her, and how he came out of his shell talking to her when he thought nobody was watching. It was something that couldn't be forced. A bond between two people that was so natural and real.

As much as I was happy for Poppy, I couldn't help but envy her. Part of me wondered what it would be like to be matched with someone that I actually loved.

"Can I tell you something?" I blurted out without thinking over what I was about to say.

I had debated on saying anything at all, but I just needed to get it off my chest. Even if I couldn't tell her the whole truth. How traitorous my thoughts really were.

"Anything," she replied as she fixed the strands of hair poking out from my up-do and fastened the silver hairpin tighter into my hair. It was a gift I had gotten for my tenth birthday from my mother. She said girls with pretty hair get picked. The bottom of the pin was engraved with my initials: *"A.R.R."*

I leaned in and whispered to her. "I am not nervous because I am scared of who I will end up with. I am nervous because… I don't think that I can live this way—"

"Amara, Poppy, you both need to be seated. Now," one of the maids demanded as she rushed out towards the other room where the ceremony was held.

"Hold that thought. We can talk more after we are matched. Don't worry, you will be fine!" she squealed and ran after the maid.

A part of me sighed in relief at the fact that I didn't get to voice how I was truly feeling. Without the interruption, I would have put her at risk for even talking about such things.

I don't know what even came over me, but I just felt like I needed to say something before my life changed forever. It wasn't fair of me though, to put that on her. It wasn't her problem, it was mine. And it would stay as *only* mine.

After all, it was why we existed. Why the matching ceremony was even put into place. We were for carrying on lineages and legacies, and the matching ensures that humans don't go extinct. *"It was an honor to even be matched,"* they told us.

Every woman that I knew seemed to think so, but I couldn't help but wonder if it was not "honorable," but really just that we were their only hope.

Honor would also imply that we had a choice. That actions were taken willingly to do the right thing. How could it be honorable if there was no other option?

As I chased after Poppy down the dimly lit halls, baritone voices sounding from down the hallway caught my attention.

I knew that voice.

I crept my face around the corner of the stone walls to see three men standing in a circle only twenty feet in front of me.

One was of Alastor, our leader. Another I recognized as Poppy's father and the third I had not heard before.

I could only make out a few words, and the ones I did hear made no sense. "We need to begin… harvest… Start with crushing them down… Will take back what—" They stopped as they sensed my looming presence. Alastor's head snapped in my direction and I resumed walking down the hallway.

Oh no.

My brisk walk quickly turned into a run as I remembered what could happen to a woman who eavesdrops. Especially on the leader of the underground. The nerves in my stomach coiled up into a tight ball.

But no matter how scared I was, I couldn't help but wonder what their conversation was about.

What had they been discussing that deserved such hushed voices?

I filed what I observed in my mind for later when I would have time to go over it. To try and figure out what they were talking about.

But in the meantime, I forced myself to forget about what I heard, and I hoped that Alastor wouldn't remember who he had seen either since the hallway was so dark.

I clung to that hope as I pushed open the heavy wooden doors to the matching hall.

2

My heart pounded against my chest so hard I thought it might be trying to claw its way out as I sat next to the few other twenty-year-old girls who had the same birthday as me. We were all waiting for our names to be called, and Poppy was a few seats ahead of me.

As children, we wished for this day to come faster. Sharing a birthday with Poppy meant that we would both be matched with our husbands on the same day. Our childish brains deemed it to be a sign that we were meant to be friends forever.

When really, it was just one of the underground traditions that when a woman turned twenty, that day they are able to be matched to the eligible men who are also twenty, *or older.*

The beating of my heart only quickened when I realized that my name was first alphabetically.

Everyone sat silently in their seats watching. Some young women had sneers on their faces and jealousy oozing out from them. They thought that us going before them would mean fewer options later when it was their turn. Not that we even got to choose anyway.

My eyes rolled at the ridiculous notion of getting mad at someone for something only fate could decide. Or in this case, *men*.

Several families were sitting in the crowd of people packed into the large room where the ceremony was held.

It was grand, with high ceilings and torches perched on the sides of each wall. A large chandelier swung from above, with candles balancing on its posts. One would think it was beautiful, but I found it plain. I couldn't find beauty in the stone walls, or the orange glow from the candles anymore, as I did when I was young.

As a child, the room felt brighter, almost as if sunlight had somehow made its way all the way underground to this square, stone room.

Now, it just felt dark. Dull. As it always had been, but somehow never felt as such when I was young. The older I became, the more depressing everything seemed.

"The first match of the day…" the speaker started in an extremely monotone voice that ironically seemed fitting. "Is Amara Raven," she finished.

I tensed before brushing my skirt with my palms and standing up in one quick movement. The few faint freckles that scattered across my nose and tops of my cheeks began to feel like a marking of a cull as I looked around at the young faces staring at me. The two other women in the chairs beside me had perfect skin. Not a blemish or a freckle to be seen. Their blonde, pin-straight hair fell down past their shoulders and glistened in the candlelight.

My hair was too unruly to be let down. The loose curls that my dark brown hair took as their natural form were deemed "messy." My hair was always brushed back into an updo for special occasions.

I seemed to float and drift across the floor to where the speaker stood, her face matching the tone of her voice. Her eyes relaxed into thin slits and her mouth into a flat line.

My body recognized the weight of that moment more than my mind did. I shook with adrenaline and something inside me screamed.

"Go."

"Go!"

"GO! RUN!"

I didn't know why or how, but ever since I was a child I had an extremely loud inner voice.

I knew that everyone had one, but mine was so loud and clear that it was hard to ignore sometimes.

It was as if my subconscious knew things that I didn't. Almost like an outside force had been speaking to me, guiding me throughout life.

It wasn't even really a voice per se, more of a feeling that turned to thoughts. Thoughts that I knew weren't solely my own, but of some gift from fate.

That is how it felt at least, but it was no coincidence that my gut feelings were *never* wrong. Any time I heard the ringing in my ears and the dull stab in my gut along with a random thought of guidance, I knew that it was the voice.

Lately, it had been even more loud than usual. It was begging me to grasp onto it. To give in to the unknown force that seemed to dwell in my veins, my blood. I ignored it.

This moment felt so painful and drained of life and light. Was it a foreshadowing of my future? To my life if I were to be chosen?

Was it some sort of warning that fate was giving me? A sign to do something to get out of it.

My thoughts were interrupted by the speaker as she said, "Now is the time for the eligible men to write down their level of interest in Amara, and whoever has the highest interest will be matched to her. Please place a number between zero and one hundred on the tally for Amara."

I nervously held my head down, too afraid to make eye contact with any of them as I heard the rustle of the piece of paper slide from man to man and then back to the speaker.

I felt as if there were eyes on me, but I wasn't going to look at who it was.

"Now the match, if any, for Amara will be revealed."

If any.

A sliver of hope beamed deep within my chest as I remembered once in a very great while, a woman is not chosen if there is no interest from any of the men.

A hope that shouldn't have been there.

What is wrong with me?

When a woman isn't chosen by any of the eligible men, they are sentenced to be a maid for the rest of their days.

Sentenced.

A punishment for not being desirable enough, when we are taught to be modest.

The few steps I made to close the gap between the speaker and myself felt like stepping stones to my execution.

The speaker cleared the phlegm from her throat as she unrolled a piece of paper and held it to the candlelight to read. "Amara does in fact have a match…"

My heart sank a bit at those seven words, but my mind was conflicted as half of me perked up at the fact that I was desirable, to one man at least.

Nausea swirled in my stomach as I admitted my pleasure mentally. As much as I did not want to be matched, I couldn't help but feel like I achieved something. Since it was what we were raised for—

To get picked. It was our one life goal being a woman in the underground and everything we were prepared for. So I couldn't help but feel a bit accomplished.

The small high that I felt was washed away quickly as I surveyed the possible men who could have chosen me. I gulped as I examined each one. I could only recognize a few that I had seen before.

I saw one was Mason, the underground leader's son. His father, Alastor was feared by most, but also highly praised by all of us. Feared because he could banish anyone at any time, but praised because he kept us safe from the outside world.

Although, it was a crime to speak badly about the leader, so no one dared to say an ill word. There wasn't anything bad to say about him anyway, since he had only ever made decisions that protected our community from what lies above.

Mason, on the other hand, was the complete opposite of what I've observed. He was just an arrogant moron who would tease and make eyes at any woman who he came in contact with.

It was a crime to bed someone before marriage, and Mason had ruined several girls' reputations by sleeping with them. It was a known fact that Mason had a way with words, and the minute after you gave yourself to him, he would pretend like you didn't exist. Many girls mistake him to be *"changing for her"* and say that *"it would be different because he said..."*

But it was always the same result.

Every. Single. Time.

It was never their fault. I couldn't blame them for believing him. I would probably have done the same if I wasn't someone on the outside looking in.

Those girls never even retaliated or became angry with him because they knew that if word got out to the higher-ups, they would be banished.

Mason, however, would never suffer any repercussions, which is why he would never stop deflowering the poor girls who believed that he truly loved them. Being the leader's son, and a man, made him untouchable. He knew that.

I said a quick prayer, to whatever gods could be listening, for the poor girl who would be matched to him.

He was disgusting, and it was a shame that no one else could see through it.

I scanned the row of men and my eyes locked upon *him*. His shaggy brown hair was swooshed to one side and the slight waves curled like they were trying to get away from his face. I didn't blame them.

Despite my dislike for Mason and how I usually recoiled at the sight of him, this time something inside me heated. I felt a burn in my throat as time seemed to stand still.

His head whipped in my direction as if he could sense my gaze upon him. My eyes connected with his, but they weren't… *his*.

His expression and the way he seemed to peer into my very soul… he never looked that way before. Never looked at *me*. And I didn't mean ogling, I mean truly looked at me. As if he could see every thought racing through my mind and every memory that I had locked away. As if he could *feel* what I was feeling.

There was some imaginary force between us that wouldn't let either of us look away and seemed to pull us together like a magnet.

I wished that I had a bucket of water to splash onto myself and then a rock to drop over my head for even letting that moment happen. I knew better than that and I sure as hell wasn't going to fall under his spell.

I closed my eyes for a few moments in an attempt to calm my traitorous heart and then looked to the seat next to him.

The other man that I knew was Sam. We had been friends since we were kids. Although I knew that he would make a great match, I didn't want him. And it was no secret that he was going to choose Poppy.

Sam was short, and even shorter now as he slouched in his chair, tapping his foot on the ground as if he too was so nervous he couldn't sit still. His glasses slipped down his nose and he quickly pushed them back up with a pointer finger to keep them from falling.

Poor thing. He looked even worse than I did. I felt bad to admit that seeing Sam so nervous made me feel a tiny bit better. The difference between us though was that he truly had nothing to worry about.

The speaker looked up in shock before she returned her eyes back to the paper and re-read it. "It seems… Amara has been chosen by Mason."

Something inside me froze over and cracked in what felt like a second. I couldn't help but let out a small grin and a breathy laugh at what felt like a sick prank from fate.

It couldn't be real.

I refused to believe that I was awake. It had to be a nightmare. I reached down and squeezed the taught skin on my forearm, hard enough to turn it red afterward.

All I felt was pain as I looked around waiting to wake up.

The gasps from the watchers filled the room and then it went completely silent. All of the parents of the eligible girls were radiating with envy.

I let out a sigh of relief when I realized I wasn't matched with Sam, at least for Poppy's sake, but I couldn't help but feel my heart sink at the thought of spending forever with Mason and being his wife.

Wife. My body broke out into full-body chills at the thought of it.

All the other girls who were turning twenty soon were radiating with jealousy, so much so that for a second I thought I could physically see waves of it rippling off of them, but *I* wished to be chosen by someone else.

Or not chosen at all.

They can have him.

I wished for nothing more than to shove him off onto someone else.

I had never even had a true, meaningful conversation with Mason, and I was unsure that he was even capable of having one based on what I had observed.

I couldn't imagine telling him about my books and him understanding them, or even just laughing with each other and enjoying each other's presence. As a matter of fact, I couldn't imagine any of those men doing those things. I pursed my lips and squinted my eyes, trying anything to picture a beautiful life that I could potentially have with Mason, but something inside of me tore the image apart and shredded it to bits.

My gut told me it wasn't right. He wasn't right. But I ignored myself, as it was all that I *could* do.

Mason walked out onto the stage with his eyes fixed on me. He was tall and lean, and his brown hair bounced in waves with each step that he took.

He stared at me, transfixed as if I was a prize that he had just won. I uncomfortably tugged on my dress to make it longer, even if it had been just a few inches.

That pull between us was even stronger as he stepped closer. And as much as I wanted to run away, my soul began to sing.

Confusion stirred in my mind as my gut feeling told me to get as far away from him as possible, but another part of me wanted to be near him.

I never had that reaction to him before in all the times that I had seen him or walked past him.

Why now?

Why at all?

"Hello, *Amara*," he said, his voice deep and rough as he enunciated my name.

"Mason." I bowed my head in an effort to hide the tension that was embedded in my face and the wetness in my eyes.

3

Mason disappeared right after the matching, even though it was common to walk arm in arm with your betrothed through the underground. A victory lap for the men to show off their new, shiny toys.

I didn't mind walking alone. However, I did mind the stares that I received because Mason wasn't by my side. Where he should've been, but also where I didn't want him to be.

I couldn't help but wonder why Mason had chosen me. He had never shown interest in me before. He probably wrote down a one and was unlucky enough to be the only one to show any interest.

It wasn't that I thought I was ugly, I just knew I wasn't good enough. I knew that I wasn't anything close to being the prettiest one in the underground. I was okay with that, but it made me wonder... *why me*?

He must have run out of girls that he hadn't already been with. Probably just bored and wanting to try me out now that there was no one else left.

Sadly, it would last longer than one time.

Poppy and Sam walked in front of me, smiling at each other with their arms interlocked. I smiled slightly at their happiness while nausea crept its way through my stomach. I *was* happy for her.

Poppy turned her head back to see me and slowed as she reached out her hand for me to hold.

"How are you doing?" she asked lowly. She knew exactly how I felt about Mason and how devastated I must have been.

"Great," I said as I felt a tear slip down my cheek. I wiped it away casually, making sure not to draw attention.

I hated that anytime someone asked me how I was or how I was doing when I was sad, it was like a dam cracking open and the emotions flowing out like rushing water. I no longer could hold back the tears.

As much as I wanted to be emotionless and act like everything was okay, my face told a different story.

"Oh, Amara," she sighed as she squeezed my hand tighter. "I am so sorry. I know he was not what you wanted—"

"It's fine." I squeezed her hand to reassure her even though it was not fine. Everything was so terribly far from being fine. I wanted to scream and cry at the same time. To run away. "It's not your fault."

It was *his*.

Why would he choose me? What was his secret agenda? I knew there had to be more than mere attraction. It didn't make any sense why he would show interest in me. I was sure that he was going to pick the blonde to my left with plump lips and the perfect form. The girl I had always seen him eyeing in the gathering spot after class. I had assumed that she was going to be his next victim unless he was tired of her already.

"If you need anything—" Poppy started, but I pulled away and put my hand to my chest.

"Poppy, it is fine. Truly, I'm fine! I am so happy for you and Sam. Do not let me ruin your day," I said with a smile so forced I was sure my cheeks would rip open.

She tilted her head sideways as if she could see right through my lies. "Fine, but later we will talk." She leaned closer to whisper to me, "I want to hear all about how you feel. Okay?"

She said it so sincerely that I felt bad for not telling her how I feel most times. It's not that I wanted to hide myself from her, I just didn't think she would understand. And my feelings weren't worth it to put her at risk.

"Okay," I agreed. She accepted my answer and then turned back to Sam with the biggest grin on her face. A true one.

True happiness beamed from both of them. Sam was the opposite of the mess he had been earlier. It was like he turned into a new person when he was in Poppy's presence. Two halves of one whole that were so bright when they came together, they shined like gold.

❀ ❀ ❀

Dinner was after the walk and Mason at least felt inclined to show up to that. The relief I felt was only so that I did not have to share the burden of interacting with my parents and his father all by myself.

The chandelier above us cast a warm glow upon the room, and the flickering of the candles reflected off the red tablecloth that stretched the length of the long wooden table. The room was filled with the sound of clinking silverware and the occasional scraping of wood chairs against the hard stone floor.

It was tradition that after the matching, the two "almost" joined families have dinner together.

I stared at my plate, picking at the food on it. It was a white mush that I assumed to be potatoes or oats. Neither enticed me anymore as they did for the first twenty years of my life, but now it was just getting old.

I stirred the food around, not feeling inclined to take a single bite even though my stomach was growling. A feeling I had gotten used to partly because I couldn't stand that tasteless gruel, and partly because it was *"un-ladylike"* and *"unbecoming"* to eat a large amount.

Everyone needed to eat to live, but apparently the women less than the men.

I looked up from my plate to find Mason's eyes pinned on me. He stared at me, *through me*, with an emotion that I could not quite place. It was that same expression that he had during the ceremony.

It was then that I noticed that there was something different about him that I didn't notice during the ceremony, probably because of how overwhelmed I was.

I had seen him many times in the gathering spot, talking to his friends or flirting with women. He always had piercing, bright blue eyes.

After spending years around the same people, I seemed to remember the smallest details about them that I didn't think I even picked up on.

It might have been the lighting, or maybe the fact I never had gotten that close to his face before, but I could've sworn his eyes were so dark that they almost looked black. The color of true darkness.

Maybe I had imagined blue eyes being so far away from him most of the time. My brain must have filled in the blanks for the details that I did not take the time to memorize.

Trying to distract myself from Mason's intense gaze, I looked around the room. The walls were cream-colored stone, but the torches and candles scattered throughout the dining room gave everything a yellow hue. The long table was adorned with metal chalices, each one catching the light in a different way. It was easier for me to look at anything else but Mason. To focus on the pattern of the tablecloth or count the number of cracks in the stone walls.

Mason gave me a knowing smile as if he could sense my discomfort. For a moment I thought he would look away, realizing how anxious he made me, but it egged him on even more, and his stare only intensified with each passing second.

He then propped his head up in the palms of his hands as his elbows rested on the table. His head cocked sideways and his mouth turned upward into an evil grin. For just a split second, I could have sworn I saw a flicker of light in his eyes. He quickly turned towards my father, angling his head away from mine. The faint silver glow disappeared from his irises just as fast as it appeared.

Alastor cleared his throat, bringing my attention back to the conversation at hand. One that I had not been a part of. Mostly by choice, partly because I had no place in it.

"We've heard great things about your family's metalworking skills, Amara," he said, taking a sip of his wine. "I am sure our joined families will be able to do great things once aligned."

I smiled nervously, grateful for the compliment but not quite sure what to say as the compliment was directed mostly at my father. He comes from a line of skilled metallurgists. Spending all day sourcing iron and other metals for the underground, he is hardly at home. Not that I cared too much.

My father was similar to that of the iron that he worked with. He was cold and rigid. It made sense that he worked with metals and rocks because he wasn't too great with people.

If I had to be honest with myself, I hated him.

He wasn't a kind man to me or my mother, not that my mother was much better to me, but he was cruel and extremely hard to be around. I cared for him in the way that you would care for a stranger. You wouldn't want anything bad to happen to them per se, but if something did happen, you would be indifferent. Neutral to their downfall.

We had no relationship whatsoever, and most times, it felt as if I was just a pawn to him. Another tool to get him what he wanted.

I was positive that he wished for a son instead. When my mother wasn't able to have another child, he turned even more cold towards me. Towards both of us.

"Yes, my father is quite skilled in precious metal sourcing as well as crafting," I replied, and my father cut me off as he began talking about his plans to mine more iron for the underground. My mind began drifting out of the conversation again.

Alastor politely returned the focus of the conversation back to me as he said "Amara, I do believe that you will make an excellent wife. Your genes… they are exquisite. Perfect for reproducing," he said dragging his gaze from my eyes down to my feet. It was so quick that no one else noticed. *I barely did.*

I didn't know why, but my stomach twisted and bile began to burn in my throat as his words settled in. No one else seemed to care.

It must be normal to be treated this way once officially twenty.

But even so, it made me feel sick. And uncomfortable. Not in the same way Mason was making me feel.

I noticed Mason glaring at his father out of the corner of my eye. He met my eyes with his and something like anger crossed over his expression.

"Thank you—"

"Well, I find it interesting, *Father*," he spat out the words like it was poison in his mouth, "that you would insinuate that reproducing is all that *she* is good for…" The entire table turned their heads toward Mason in shock. "Especially since I haven't seen you do anything but *reproduce* lately." He clicked his tongue.

I stifled back a laugh with a cough into my arm and Mason smiled wide.

Alastor had been busy as he had several illegitimate children born from several different women. They were all much younger than Mason but ranged in age from newborns to young teens.

Seems like his father also liked to fool around with multiple women.

Like father like son.

The only difference was that Alastor had a wife. Although it was a crime for women to bed before marriage, people looked the other way when men did it. It made no sense to me. Especially since it takes two. How could women be more at fault than men for simply doing the same thing?

"Excuse me?" Alastor ground out, and it was clear that he was genuinely stunned by his son's response.

"You heard me, *Father*." Mason casually picked up a spoonful of gruel and licked it off with his tongue in a motion that could be considered downright obscene.

My stomach dropped at the movement.

His face curled into disgust as if it was the worst thing he had ever tasted, and then spit it into a napkin.

"I would've spit that into your face, but unlike you, I have table manners," he said clinking the spoon onto his plate and then dragged his eyes to meet mine and picked up the knife next to his plate. "And the next time you look at her that way… you won't be able to *look* at anything else again," he said as he stabbed a small circular loaf of bread next to him. The knife stood up on its own as he pulled his arms into his chest and crossed them.

Alastor's face twisted in confusion. "Mason, are you feeling alright? You don't seem quite… yourself."

"I'm perfect." He rolled his eyes and sat back lazily in his chair. "Now, let's talk more about these… *plans.*"

"Yes, agreed! It is the way of the world, anyway, isn't it?" my father replied in a sad attempt to lighten the mood. My mother's head spun to face my father's. She seemed inclined to yell at my father the way Mason had just yelled at Alastor. Hope festered within at the thought of her standing up for me, but it dissipated as she frowned and faced back toward her meal.

As we finished dinner, I excused myself to use the bathroom, hoping for a few moments of solitude to pull myself together as knots twisted in my stomach.

I closed my eyes and hoped that I could reverse time to be a child again. Hazy images and visions appeared in my head of memories from when I was young, with no care in the world and no duties to fulfill. I knew I wasn't ready for marriage, but there was nothing I could do.

A loud knock interrupted the deep thoughts I had spiraled into. My shallow breaths became more drawn out as I worked to calm myself down.

"Just a minute!" I called out, inhaling deeply.

As I opened the door, Mason stood in front of me, his arms crossed as he leaned against the doorway. His eyes trained on my lips, tracking every movement like a bloodhound. "Are... You alright?" he asked, his voice straining as if it was an effort to care.

I took a step back, feeling the heat rise in my cheeks. "I'm fine," I replied, attempting but failing to keep my voice even.

The effect he had on me was strange. I couldn't wrap my head around the fact that I had seen him several times over the years, even spoken to him, and I never once felt the connection between us that existed right then.

Never before did my breathing become ragged solely because of his presence.

There was the magnetic feeling again—as if our very two souls were cut from the same cloth and begged to be sewn back together.

No. I pushed that feeling down, down, down until it was gone. I didn't know what it had meant and I didn't care either.

Mason leaned in closer, his breath hot against my neck. "I didn't mean to embarrass you. I am just protective over what's mine," he whispered.

What's mine?

There was that arrogance, however it was fueled by a cunning sort of charming nature rather than true possessiveness. As if he solely wanted to get a rise out of me, and that was the only goal.

I shoved his face away, my heart racing. "I have to get back to dinner," I said, my voice shaking. "Excuse me." I pushed past him, but he made his way to step in front of me, blocking the entrance to the hallway.

His hand softly gripped my arm and as he did, his eyes locked onto me. Not in the way they had at the dinner table, but as if he was assessing me. It was like he could see into my soul like he was reading a page of a book that was *me*.

His head tilted as he furrowed his eyebrows. "Interesting."

My eyes widened as I glanced around his face for answers. "What?" I breathed.

Part of me wondered if he had felt it too. That pull between us. The force that begged us to be closer.

The skin where his hand gripped my arm felt like molten lava as his touch seared into me like an invisible brand planting its roots through my veins.

He silently continued staring. His face was the epitome of calm.

Something in me snapped at the fact he refused to explain himself to me. "Well, if you are just going to stand here and stare at me all day, remember this image in your mind for later, because I am leaving," I blurted as I ripped my arm from his grasp and pushed my way past him.

As soon as the words came out of my mouth, the frustration was replaced by fear of what could happen if Mason told Alastor how blunt I was to my *soon-to-be husband.*

I was too stubborn to apologize though.

I could be banished.

The internal war with myself was stopped short as he let out a laugh that seemed to be guided by approval.

Although I hated to admit it, his utter delight at my rudeness sent a rush of warmth through my veins.

4

The heavy wooden door creaked as I pushed it open, revealing the dark and damp hallway that led to my chambers. The stone walls were cold to the touch, and the torches that lined the hallway cast shadows that flickered and danced across the stone surface. The sound of my footsteps echoed through the empty hallway, bouncing off the walls and filling the space with an eerie sense of loneliness, as it usually did.

As I made my way down the hallway, I couldn't help but think about the stark contrast between how the rest of the underground looked compared to my bedroom.

The outside of my living quarters was made of the same rough-hewn stone as the rest of the commune, and torches were mounted on either side of the heavy wooden door. Once inside, and in my room, however, the atmosphere was much more inviting than the rest of the underground. My room was full of life, while the world outside of it was the complete opposite.

My room was a bright shade of white, not like the cream color of the stone walls in the rest of the dwelling. I begged for a different color for one of my birthdays, and my mother settled on white. I was happy enough to just have another color to set it apart. Even if it was still plain and neutral.

Elegant wooden furniture was scattered throughout with gold embellishments and there were candles everywhere. Their soft glow provided an orange tint that lit up my space. I also had red roses scattered around in vases, tacked on the wall, and placed around my golden-framed mirror.

Roses were my favorite flower. I've liked them since I was a child when I learned that I shared a middle name with them.

But even as I tried to focus on the familiar comforts of my living quarters, my mind kept wandering back to Alastor's conversation that I had overheard before the matching. My curiosity got the better of me as I ran through different explanations of what they could have possibly been referring to.

I couldn't think of anything. Nothing that made sense at least. It upset me more than it should have, and then I forced myself to give up.

My thoughts ran rampant trying to get away from my failure to figure out what I had heard, and landed on Mason. On the way, he acted during dinner. He seemed different than usual.

Arrogant as all hell, that was the same. But mixed in with the arrogance was a *wonder*. I could see the wheels in his head turning in a way that I had not noticed before.

Deep thoughts were never something I assumed Mason to ever have. The Mason that I knew would have never stood up for me that way either.

But then he had to go and ruin it by calling me *his*. Even though I was technically *his*, it upset me. I didn't like the thought of being someone's property, but that was something I needed to get used to.

I was utterly annoyed by Mason's very presence, but I couldn't stop thinking about that strange feeling I had around him.

Maybe it was just my body trying to trick itself into thinking Mason was someone I *wanted* to be around. I wouldn't put it past myself to subconsciously make him seem more desirable to avoid being miserable.

Then there was another feeling that appeared, and it was worse than how I felt for Mason.

Dread began to swirl in my core as I realized the weight that was on my shoulders. Not just for myself, but for my family.

If I were to somehow screw up the engagement, I would be ruined. My reputation would be tarnished and my family name would be disgraced. Even if I did nothing wrong, if Mason just *decided* that he didn't want me anymore, it would be viewed as *my* fault.

Everyone would assume that I had done something to make him decide otherwise.

The worst part about it was that I actually had done something wrong. Even though Mason seemed thrilled at my behavior, he could still turn around and ruin everything. And given how sick in the head he is, he would do it just for fun.

I knew that I had to make sure this worked. I had to win him over. Convince him that I would be the perfect wife. That I would be worth marrying.

I had to convince him that I was someone who wouldn't bore him.

I plucked one of the roses that lined the frame of my mirror. The petals were soft against my fingertips.

I brought the flower to my nose and took in the musky aroma. As the scent soothed my anxiety, a thought appeared in my mind. A plan to ensure this union would not fail. Probably not a great one or one that I would even be comfortable doing, but one that would work.

A plan that also might reveal anything about Alastor and what he had been talking about with Poppy's father. I knew it was none of my business, but I couldn't control myself from wondering what their secret was. What they are hiding from the rest of the underground.

I wanted to know.

I would be killing two birds with one stone, or so I convinced myself.

I slipped on my white robe, the linen fabric brushed against my skin. I then pulled the pin from my hair, letting it fall onto my back in a way I never usually wore it.

Well, a way that the maids did not allow it to be worn because it was *"improper."*

Using my fingers, I brushed my hair a bit, which seemed to only make it look even more messy. The constant touching of my soft curls made them uncoil. I groaned but decided it would have to do. I didn't have time to reshape them with water and a bit of wax to tame them.

As quietly as possible, I slowly pulled open the wooden door of my bedroom. My head peeked around the corner, peering into the dark hallway that led to the front door of our chambers.

At such a late hour my parents had to be sleeping, so it wasn't a concern. Waking them up was my fear.

I tip-toed down the hallway cringing every time my feet brushed against the stone floor too loud.

Ten feet.

My heart pounded faster with every step that I took.

Five feet.

Almost there.

Two feet.

My hand reached for the handle, and just as my hand grazed the metal latch locking the door, a familiar voice stopped me dead in my tracks.

"Amara," my mother sighed. I did not even have to look at her to know that her arms were crossed and a cold expression took over her face.

I spun around towards her. My mouth gaped open and my eyes widened.

"I—"

"Where do you think you are going?" she cut me off. The dim lighting of the hallway made her seem even more stern than usual. At night, there are only a few candles that stay lit.

Her dark hair was pulled back into an updo that was comfortable for sleeping. The light illuminated her sharp facial features and her frail body.

"I was going to see Poppy," I lied.

"Lies. You hardly even see Poppy in the daytime with your head always buried in those books. Where. Are. You. Going," she demanded.

"Mother, I—" I frowned.

"The truth, Amara!" she barked, but still quiet enough so that my father wouldn't wake up.

The truth?

I wasn't sure I would still be breathing if I gave her the truth. But what choice did I have? My mother always knew when I was lying. Somehow.

I sighed. "I was going to—to see Mason," I said as I made eye contact with her.

"Mason?" Her lips tightened and her brows furrowed. "Why?"

"I was afraid that I had been rather…" An audible gulp escaped from me. "…Quiet at dinner. I did not want him to think he was about to marry a boring woman. I was going to try and impress him. The honor of our family is the most important thing to me, and I thought maybe if I showed him that I could be the wife he wanted he wouldn't want anyone else. I would—we would be safe." My chest heaved as I explained the truth. What I could tell her of it at least.

It was true that I needed to make sure Mason still wanted me, but I left out the part about wanting to spy for more information about what Alastor was hiding.

My mother was silent for a few moments as her eyes examined me from head to toe.

"Dressed like that?" She motioned to the robe that covered only the parts I wouldn't want exposed. "Was that your way of *impressing* him?"

"Yes," I admitted and now it felt dumb to even think such a thing would work based on the way she was glaring at me.

"Hm," she grunted. "Well, go impress him then."

"What?" I responded. I fully expected her to banish me herself after understanding what I was planning to do.

"He is to be your *husband* Amara. Go impress him, by all means."

I wasn't quite sure why, but my heart sank at her words. Although I was happy to not be in trouble, I wasn't expecting encouragement.

I turned back around to face the door, my hand gripping the handle.

"You are right. If you do not succeed in this marriage, you will fail me. Do not disgrace this family. Do what you need to do."

I stood there for a few long moments as I listened to her footsteps fade down the hallway.

My eyes burned as I flung open the door and shut it forcefully behind me. I wasn't bothering to be quiet anymore.

I started down another dark hallway passing by several different living quarters of families in the underground.

The gathering spot was in the middle of the community. It was an area where people… *gather*. It was desolate that time of night. Every single table was empty, not a soul to be seen.

I had to pass through there to get to Mason and Alastor's living quarters which were on the direct opposite side that mine were on.

The underground was fairly large, so it took around a half hour to walk to the middle and another twenty minutes to walk to his living quarters from the gathering spot.

It took me even longer to get there because I had to walk as slowly as possible so that the guards wouldn't hear me. When the unmarried women are caught outside of our dwellings after curfew, we could get sent to sleep in the jail for a few nights to teach us a lesson.

I didn't want to end up in a jail cell, so I sacrificed my time and decided to be as careful as possible not to get caught. Even if it took me a ridiculous amount of time to get there.

As I finally neared Mason's dwelling, my heart stopped at the figure standing outside. As I got closer I realized *who* exactly was planted outside the front door, sitting as if he was waiting for someone.

"Well, this is unexpected." Mason grinned.

5

Although it was dark, I could make out the features of Mason's face as I neared the front of his dwelling. The closer I came, the more obvious it was that his eyes were indeed blue, not the inky black color that my mind thought them to be earlier.

So I was right?

"Your eyes," I breathed.

"My eyes?" he snarled. "You came all the way here to tell me that I have eyes? Thank you, this has been wonderful." He turned to head back inside.

"No, that's not why I came," I said, startled at his tone of voice and how opposite it was from dinner. I reached for his arm. I let my confusion slip away as I remembered what I came here to do.

His head rotated just enough so that his eyes could fixate on me. "Then why did you come?" He licked his lips as if he could sense where this was going. Or at least where he wanted it to go.

I fiddled with my fingers and my chest heaved as I attempted to speak. Nothing would come out. The more I stumbled the more interested he became. Something in me recoiled at that, but I forced myself to respond.

"I want to have fun," I said as I allowed the right side of my robe to slip down my shoulder.

His eyes darted toward the skin that lay bare. He might as well have been drooling as his mouth gaped open and his pupils dilated.

Disgusting.

He was so easily distracted it was like dangling a slab of meat in front of a dog. Thankfully for me, it would make everything easier, and it would keep him from suspecting the other reason why I was there.

The *real* reason I was there if I had to admit it to myself. Yes, I wanted to protect our family name, but my curiosity was the true motive.

My heart was pounding so fast I could audibly hear each beat. It wasn't beating this time from Mason, it was because of nerves. The possibility of getting caught.

With a gust of courage, I whispered his name, "Mason," in a soft tone. My feet moved quicker than my mind could process as I took a step forward and placed my hand on his chest. "Do you want me to show you *why* you chose correctly?"

"And I was starting to think you would be boring," he said, trailing his fingers down the length of my back. His touch felt like acid, making my skin crawl in disgust. I was itching to run home and wipe off every patch of skin that he grazed.

He is to be your husband Amara. Go impress him, by all means.

The words of my mother echoed into my head every time I had the inkling to run away. Every time I internally shivered while he touched me.

The way he had been talking earlier at dinner, it was charming.

It was all an act.

An effort to convince me that he wasn't all that bad. Maybe even to get me there, to that moment.

That was the Mason I knew. The one who would make a girl very unlucky someday.

That girl was me.

I didn't say anything back, I didn't need to. What I was about to do would speak for itself.

I reached for the tie on my robe and pulled one of the strings ever so slightly. The garment began to slide off my shoulders and then down my legs, straight to the floor. I was now standing in just my undergarments in front of Mason.

His eyes roamed up and down my body. I could physically feel his gaze as if it were a knife dragging across my body.

He took my hand into his and led me inside.

No one was ever awake at these hours, so I wasn't worried about being seen.

That thought sparked my interest as to why Mason was even awake. Standing outside for that matter.

"Why were you up this late?" I whispered as we made our way through his dwelling.

I could practically feel his eyes roll as he let out a huff and responded gruffly. "Took a nap earlier. Couldn't sleep."

"When did you have time to take a nap? We have been at the matching ceremony all day—"

He yanked me towards him as we entered the room near the front of the dwelling. It looked the same as any other place in the underground. Dark. Stone walls. Torches.

He plopped down onto his bed and stretched his arms behind his head.

"Let's see if you're all talk." He motioned to his lower half.

I wanted to slap him. Every bone in my body wanted to yell at him. I wasn't sure why either. This is what we are prepared for.

I decided to use it to my advantage. I figured that in his state of desire, he wouldn't be suspicious of me.

"Where is your father?" I asked as I traced a single finger down from his chest to his stomach.

His eyes were glued to my hand, and his voice filled with annoyance. A mix of pleasure and frustration swirled in his expression.

"Don't know. Probably at a meeting—"

So he isn't here…

"Please don't mention my father, it's really killing the mood." He rolled his eyes and then readjusted his body to be more comfortable.

"Right… I'm sorry," I said, drawing circles around his belly button. "Just one more thing…"

Make it count Amara.

"He isn't home, but the curfew was four hours ago. Why would he have a meeting in the middle of the night and not during the day?"

That would tell me all I needed to know. If he truly was at a meeting at this time, it meant that he didn't want those who he was meeting with to be seen. If it was just a normal meeting, it could be during the day and no one would think it was strange.

I then thought of Poppy's father and how I didn't find it odd that he was meeting with him. Her father, from what little I knew about him, was skilled in botany. I wasn't sure how his skills could be beneficial to Alastor or why they had to speak in secret.

"I don't know, Amara. He has meetings during the night sometimes; it is easier that way because things are busy during the daytime. Why the interest in my father's whereabouts?" he asked, tilting his head up slightly to view my face.

"I just wanted to make sure he wouldn't be back for a while." I smiled wide as I drew my hand lower. "I wouldn't want to get you in trouble."

At least I got my answer.

Alastor was at a secret meeting and my guess was it was with Poppy's father.

"You would be the only one in trouble," he said, closing his eyes. "I'm growing bored."

I couldn't decide who I hated more. Mason or myself.

Or this place.

I hated myself for having my mind. I couldn't get out of it or escape it for just one day. I couldn't understand why I was made to have such an unruly brain that rejects reality. No one else thought this way. The other women in this place would *kill* to be in my position right now. Their minds wouldn't be whispering blasphemous ideas to them.

Why can I not stop myself from thinking of more? Even though there wasn't more.

It was time for the second part of this plan. The part I was not excited about.

I shut down my thoughts as I let my palms lay flat over his chest.

Mason looked down at my hands and then slowly looked up at me.

I could see the attraction in his eyes and I knew he wanted me. A primal instinct of mere attraction. It was too bad I couldn't return the feelings.

Physically, I could pretend to match what he was projecting. Internally, I had bile swimming up my throat.

He grabbed the back of my head and pulled me in just close enough so that I could feel his warm breath enter my mouth.

As he neared my lips I felt a nudge in my gut, and then my brain. A sharp pain struck the nerves in my head as if it were lightning touching down to the ground.

"You don't want this. He isn't for you."

"He isn't for you."

The last part repeated over and over again as if an alarm bell was going off in my head.

"Stop," I said to him and pushed away.

He pulled me in closer, thinking it was some sort of game that we had been playing.

"Stop," I repeated a bit louder, pulling away. I could sense the smile on his face as he brushed his lips against mine.

"*Stop!*" I screamed, pushing him away.

I could feel a lump form in my throat as my embarrassment got the better of me. Without a word, I grabbed my robe and ran out of his room and then out of his dwelling.

But as soon as I cleared the front door, Mason ran out after me and crossed his arms.

"She's breaking curfew!" he screamed. An attempt to get back at me for not giving him what he desired.

I picked up my pace and sprinted down the hallway. Before I could make it all but twenty steps, a guard appeared around the corner and grabbed me.

I glanced back at Mason as he shouted out to the guards. "Take her away."

"Are you serious?" I panted back to Mason.

"I am his betrothed." I turned to the guard gripping my arm. I pulled away as if I could wriggle out of his grip.

The guard said, dragging me by my arm. "You're not married yet."

"Mason, please! Don't let them do this," I pleaded.

Mason's attention turned to a figure appearing out of the shadows. His mood lightened as a blonde woman with plump lips came into view.

The one I had been sitting next to at the matching.

The one Mason was *actually* waiting for.

She smiled wide as he reached his hand out to her and led her inside. He threw one final glance my way and then shrugged.

A shrug. That was all he could muster up in response. All because I refused to please him. That was all I was worth to him. As if he was brushing dust off of his shoulders.

That was all I was to him.

A shrug.

I felt something dark tug at my insides. An invitation and a request. It begged me to respond. To give in. It swirled around inside of me like it was testing me out before it slipped away.

I gave up struggling and accepted my fate of spending that night, and possibly more, in a jail cell.

6

I woke up the next morning with my back pressed up against a damp stone wall. The cold seeped into my skin like a droplet of ink in water. It spread over me until goose flesh was covering every inch of my body.

I looked to my left to see iron bars in front of me, blocking me from leaving.

I hoped it had all been a bad dream and that I would wake up in my bed, but I was still in that jail cell.

To pass the time, and to calm my nerves, I counted the cracks on the wall in front of me over and over again, getting the same number every time.

"One hundred and four," I sighed.

I stood up and looked through the bars to see if the guards had still been there. I wanted to scream at them to let me out, but I figured that it wouldn't help my cause and that I should just keep my mouth shut.

All of a sudden, I heard the front gate open and the sound of clinking metal became louder until the same guard who had arrested me, and a man whom I had never seen before, were passing by my cell.

The man was tall, taller than anyone I had ever seen before. He had tousled silver hair that shined like how I would imagine the moon to shine or rays of sun reflecting off water.

His gaze met mine as they passed me, and it was a struggle not to get lost in those eyes.

His eyes. They were so captivating in their yellow color that seemed to be made from melted-down gold. I wondered what it would be like to stare into them for hours, and if I would ever want to look away.

I had never seen eyes like his before. It had to be the lighting that made them seem golden as I had never seen anyone with those colored eyes. *Blue, green, grey, brown,* but never gold.

He quickly pulled his head away and looked forward to the cell in front of mine where he would reside.

The guard threw him to the ground before he spat on him and slammed the metal door shut, walking away in disgust.

The man grimaced and wiped his face with his forearm.

"When am I going to be let out of here?" I gripped the bars of my cell and politely asked the guard as he made his way back to the front of the prison. I even batted my eyes at him as a last resort.

"I don't know. I am sure once the father of your betrothed is back from his meeting with the other side of the underground he will demand for your release." He scoffed in annoyance.

Unless Mason gets to him first and asks to retract his marriage offer.

"You don't seem happy for someone who's engaged," I heard from the opposite side of the room.

I looked up at the man sitting in the cell across from me. It was then that I noticed his colorful clothing: a white button-up with gold buttons and embellishments that swirled around in a pattern. His pants matched the shirt in the sense that they were white with golden swirls that seemed to curl around his legs. Golden boots were stretched out in front of him that matched the details of his clothing.

Then I noticed the markings on his skin. Green vines swirled around his wrists and up his fingers like tattoos.

"Excuse me?" I responded, taken back trying not to look amazed by his different clothing and markings. No one in the underground had skin markings and we rarely had colored fabrics.

"The guard said 'your betrothed' and your entire body tensed up," he clarified.

I froze and furrowed my brows at him.

"You do not love him?" he asked as he twirled an orange leaf between his fingers. His tone was so sincere that I assumed he was genuinely asking.

He spoke so confidently that I was convinced he could read my thoughts. Or maybe it had been painfully obvious from the look on my face what I truly thought of my betrothed.

"Why are you getting married to a man you do not love?" He interrupted my reflections with another question. A question that wasn't really a question. It was more of a statement than anything.

As if he did not know that it was what everyone did, except for the rare few like Poppy and Sam who actually did love each other. For everyone else, it was a matter of reproducing for the good of the human race and producing heirs for the good of your family line. To be remembered and honored.

"Why don't *you* mind your business?" I snapped back at him and turned back to the brick wall to restart the count.

One, two, three... I began again.

"But yours is quite entertaining," he shrugged.

His demeanor was so light. It intrigued me how he could be so… happy. That annoyed me even more.

"Besides, things work much differently above, and it's interesting to observe what goes on down here." His face turned grim.

I stopped dead in my tracks in the middle of my counting and spun my head back towards him.

"You are from above?" I asked, nearly shaking as I slid back towards the wall furthest from him.

He cracked a faint smile and then let his eyes meet mine. "Not quite the evil creature you were expecting?"

A smile painted over his face, not one of cunning or cruel nature, but one you would think someone to have when pleased. He seemed as if *cunning* was not even in his vocabulary.

Nevertheless, I froze and then felt rage boil up to the surface of my skin like molten lava. I remembered all the stories that my parents had told me about the beautiful-looking monsters from above and how one had killed my ancestor. Their beauty is a lure that pulls in humans.

She had been tricked by their magic and thought she was in love with one. Then, the monster lured her back to his cave and killed her in cold blood. Those senseless evil creatures who live above were capable of anything, and I wasn't going to be dumb enough to fall into one of their traps.

The smiles and the kind demeanor had to be some sort of trick to deceive me.

Little did he know, I was not easy to trust and even less easy to trick.

"You're exactly what I dreamed of. Even more hideous than I could imagine," I snarled at him.

A lie. But I was not about to tell him he was more beautiful than any man in the underground. It was something I didn't want to admit to him or even to myself.

I was not going to tell him how his eyes seemed to cast spells on me as I felt hypnotized into looking at them. Nor was I going to tell him how his form was nothing like I had seen before, or how his smile was the most warm and inviting I had ever seen.

No, I wasn't going to tell him any of that. Because the truth was, no matter how kind he seemed, I knew exactly what he was.

A monster.

I didn't know what he was capable of, and I surely didn't want to find out.

However, I was not going to treat him like he wasn't a monster in hopes of being spared. I knew what his kind was capable of. With their magic and lust for blood, they are a species to fear.

Don't show that you're scared.

Panic set through my entire body right after I told myself not to do just that. I was so frightened that I thought the small morsels of food that I had been served would come up.

We didn't speak of magic underground. It was something everyone knew not to even mention. Something so evil that even speaking about it could attract its presence. Attract *them*. We called them monsters and evil creatures to speak of them as vaguely as possible.

So we never took the chance. Never mentioned magic, never said their name.

Because no one spoke of them, I never knew what they even called themselves. Part of me wanted to ask him, but I figured that if we were never told their names, there must be a reason. There must have been a power in saying it.

In our classes, they taught us about the creatures above and how grateful we should be for our ancestors who ran to the underground. How without the leaders who decided that we move, the human race would have died off. They mentioned the people with magic as being ruthless cunning, and evil.

His smile fell, but just as quickly as it fell it grew to be wider than before.

"You're lying," he said as if he could feel that I truly didn't believe the words I had just spoken about him being hideous.

I ignored him and then continued back to counting my bricks. "One... two...three..." I muttered.

"One hundred and four," he stated matter-of-factly. His mouth was flat and his eyes held no expression.

"How? How did you know that—?"

I stopped myself before showing him any awe.

Instead, I decided to get some answers.

"How did you get captured by the underground? Why are you here?" I knew it was risky to ask those sorts of questions, but I needed to know. I was too curious for my own good.

It also seemed highly unlikely that a magical and powerful being could be trapped by humans and taken prisoner. It didn't make any sense. If they were supposed to be feared and were deadly to humans, then how was he captured by them?

"It's not like you would believe me if I told you." He ripped the leaf that he had been holding in half then crinkled the remnants up into a dust that fell from his palm.

He was right. I was taught never to trust the beings from above. Anything they say could just be a ploy or a part of a bigger plan to cause us harm.

I didn't respond. I only shrugged in agreement and stared him directly in the eyes. I wouldn't back down. I wouldn't cower and beg him to answer me. I wasn't like his kind. I didn't need to lie, trick, or manipulate people into giving me what I wanted.

"Hm." He stared at me, his eyes scanning me like I was an acquaintance that he had forgotten of until now.

"What?" I asked.

He opened his mouth as if he was about to speak when the guard came in and sauntered over to my cell.

"You're free to go, Amara," the guard stated as he slid open my cell door.

"Amara," the man repeated to himself, so quiet that if I didn't know better, I could assume that it was just the sound of a soft exhale.

I sprang to my feet and with merriment and then walked out from my cell and past the man not bothering to glance back at him.

I felt a brush against my shoulder as if someone was moving behind me. I whipped my head around, but only found him sitting in the same position he had been in the whole time.

His hand flicked up into a relaxed wave as I was led down the hallway. I struggled to pull my eyes away from him and turned back around wondering why it was so hard to do so.

❁ ❁ ❁

As I trudged my way toward the gathering spot to return to my chambers, I saw Mason surrounded by a group of women fawning over him. They piled around and looked like they were about to start fighting over who should get his attention.

He caught my glance and then smirked at me as he continued flirting.

They can have him.

I rolled my eyes and kept walking, not bothering to give Mason a second thought. I had been far too tired from the lack of sleep that I didn't have it in me to be angry. I didn't have time for it either.

Although, I *did* have time to fear whether or not Mason had told his father about what happened, or if he took back his interest in me.

There were so many possibilities of things that could go wrong, all of them ending in me getting punished, or worse, banished.

As I was about to make my way out of the gathering area, a hand yanked my arm back, spinning me around.

I was half ready to punch whoever it was right in the face until I realized who it was and let out a sigh of relief. My body calmed at the sight of her.

"Poppy," I breathed.

"I meant to catch up with you last night, but I couldn't find you. Where did you disappear off to?" she asked.

I debated on lying for a moment, but I was so sleep-deprived and stressed that I just needed someone to talk to instead of tiptoeing around in my own mind for once.

"I made a mistake." My voice broke as I choked up.

"Oh, Amara." She took my hand and led me down the dark hall to the living quarters so that we could have a moment alone. "What happened?"

I broke down and told her all of it. Everything.

Well, not *everything*. I told her what I had done the night prior and how I was captured, but I didn't mention the conversation I overheard or how that was another reason I went to see Mason.

I also left out the part about the thoughts I had been having because even just speaking about it would put both of us at risk.

"I'm so sorry," she said rubbing the side of my arm in an effort to comfort me. "And not to make matters worse, but…"

"But what?" My stomach sank to the floor as I felt that my problems were about to become much worse.

"It's Mason," Poppy began to say, hesitating. "He's telling everyone how you came to see him last night and how he thought you were going to be just another hookup." She winced as if it pained her to even say.

"A hookup? I am to be his *wife*?"

"I know, but he says he doesn't remember why he picked you. He is saying that it was almost like you used…" She looked both ways and then leaned in before she finished. "Magic." She whispered it so softly that I could barely catch what she said.

"Magic?" I was so taken aback she had to hush me to keep my voice down. "That's absurd!" I whispered back.

"I know, I know. Anyone who knows you would agree, but he doesn't, and his flock seems to believe him. They are saying that you bewitched him into choosing you."

"That doesn't even make sense! I'm human, how could they possibly think that? We don't have magic!" I said, slapping my palm to my forehead, and began pacing back and forth.

"That's why they're calling you a witch. They don't understand it, and they don't want to. They won't even accept the possibility that Mason is terrible and wants to ruin your life because you didn't give him what he wanted," she said, fixing my hair and then gripping my shoulders.

"What do I do," I looked into her eyes as I felt mine begin to burn. "If this gets back to Alastor that I bewitched his son, I will be banished—"

"Don't talk like that. Don't even say that. We will figure this out. I will talk to Mason and fix everything," she assured me. I wondered what use it would do but then I remembered she and Mason were friends as children. Maybe their childhood would mean something to him.

And with their father's secret meetings, maybe that meant their families were still close.

I wanted to ask her about it and see if she knew anything, but I knew it wasn't the right time.

"Okay," I agreed. "Thank you."

"Of course. Now, get home and get some rest."

She gave me a gentle hug before I continued my walk back.

All I could think about the whole way there was if those rumors would be the thing to get me banished and how ironic it would be that the one thing that *wasn't* true would be what landed me in trouble.

Not the sneaking out, eavesdropping on the leader's conversation, being rude to my future husband, or having traitorous thoughts about the matching and our entire way of life in general.

No, it would be the fact that I was *"a witch."*

I had finally made it back, and when I reached my bed, my body collapsed over top of the blankets.

I didn't even have the energy to get under the covers, and there wasn't even time to debate it as I drifted off the second my head touched the pillow.

❀ ❀ ❀

I awoke to a blood-curdling scream coming from the kitchen as a loud thud echoed through my dwelling.

A female voice shouted. "What did she do? Why are you taking her?"

Her?

It was then that I realized the woman screaming had been my mother.

My door busted down and four guards made their way to my bed, dragging me to the floor. One of them aggressively yanked my hands behind my back and secured them with iron chains. "What's going on? I didn't do anything wrong. Alastor already let me out for breaking curfew!" I hissed.

"This has nothing to do with you breaking curfew," one of the guards snapped back as they dragged me away while my mother was standing near the doorway.

Another guard pulled out metal chains and began to bind my hands together.

Everything had gone terribly wrong so fast.

I trusted Poppy to save me. I put blind faith in her and believed that she could influence that wretched human being, Mason.

As if he had feelings and would sympathize with me.

I can't believe I thought that it could work. I was so exhausted that morning that I hadn't even thought it over. I wasn't even capable of thinking of a better plan.

And now it would cost me.

How much, I was too afraid to admit that I already knew the cost.

Terror consumed me, but I only let it show through my eyes. I didn't cry or scream or beg them to let me go.

I wouldn't balk.

I looked at my mother and replayed her scream through my head. As if she truly did care for me, that one moment could have changed everything. I would have forgiven her cold nature and how she constantly made me feel inferior my entire life.

I would forget it all if she would just do *something*. Just once.

I made eye contact with her hoping she would recognize the silent plea for help written in my eyes.

"What have you done Amara?" Her fright quickly turned to disappointment as she sneered at me while I was taken from my bedroom. She shook her head in disbelief.

My heart cracked in two. The pain in my chest was much worse than the pain of the chains that chafed my wrists.

My mother was the first one to break eye contact as she turned and retreated into our dwelling. *Her* dwelling. A home that never felt like mine to begin with.

The door slammed with her exit.

For the first time in my life, I accepted the hard truth that my mother was the one who gave birth to me, but that was all she would ever be.

7

My heart sank all the way to my stomach by the time I arrived at the room where the guards took me.

It was a wide open room with a podium and four rows of wooden benches behind it. There was another stand on the opposite side of the room parallel with the other one.

I knew exactly what that place was.

It was where the rule breakers were tried for their crimes. Anyone who has ever entered that room has only left one way and one way only.

They led me to the smaller stand across from where Alastor was seated in the larger one. Deep wrinkles were etched on his cheeks and forehead with his eyes sunken and dark circles underneath. His expression twisted into something haunting as he noticed my presence.

I was pushed down into the wooden chair and I squirmed a bit trying to get comfortable as my hands were still stuck behind me in chains.

The room began to fill with everyone I knew. My father, Poppy, Sam, and Mason, along with other people from the underground who I did not know well enough to name, but knew they were nosey enough to come watch.

Everyone except for my mother.

Mason was standing with his arms crossed and an arrogant smile plastered across his face, but his eyes were shadowed with confusion.

I looked over to Poppy and as if she knew where this was headed, she mouthed, *"I will miss you. I am so sorry… Talked to Mason. He didn't care to tell on you."*

We had become exceptionally skilled at lip reading since we were never allowed to speak in class. The teachers were so strict we would get cracked on the hands with a ruler for even a whisper. We practiced as children and thought it would be like a secret language since no one else could do it as well as we could.

As cruel as Mason was, he would have just told the truth. He wouldn't have lied because he truly did not care enough to act like he did something when he didn't.

So why was I there?

"I will miss you too," I mouthed back to her. *"Don't forget about me."* A burn began to sting my eyes.

"Never." She winked as she wiped away the single tear that rolled down her cheek.

That's what I loved about Poppy. She never wasted time on things that didn't matter. She didn't waste our last moments of seeing each other on asking what else I had done to be in that position. Because it didn't matter what I had done. Not to her.

I didn't even know what I had done.

I mean, I eavesdropped on the leader, but he would have banished me sooner if he knew it was me.

If it wasn't anything to do with Mason, then I had no idea what else it could be.

The room went dead silent as Alastor began to speak.

"I am going to give you one chance and one chance only to admit to your crimes," Alastor said in an eerily calm voice that heightened my nerves more than if he had been screaming.

"I am sorry, but I don't know what you're talking about." I was surprised that when my words came out, it wasn't a weak tone of voice that spoke them. It was a gallant one. I wasn't sure where it came from, but I embraced it.

"Do not play dumb with me!" His entire demeanor switched as he screamed and slammed his fist on the table in response.

"You helped that wretched monster escape. You helped him to walk free when his kind have committed unspeakable acts against humans, our people, YOUR people!"

My mind felt as if it was running circles around my head trying to think about what he could have been referring to.

Escape.

He must have been talking about the prison.

At first, I couldn't remember seeing another prisoner in the ten hours I spent in that cell, but then I recalled that strange man that I had met who twirled a single leaf between his fingers with the strange ivy markings on his wrists.

I was so exhausted and thankful to be out of prison that I hadn't allowed my mind to think about him anymore.

That creature, that *man*. He looked to be the furthest thing from a beast. He seemed human and was probably the most beautiful one I had seen thus far.

But looks are deceiving. He was one of *them*.

"I did not help him escape, I had no reason to," I said firmly with no hesitation or stutter in my voice.

"How do you suppose I could have even done that from the cell I was locked in? Do you think that

I suddenly could walk through metal bars and magically be able to unlock another jail cell?"

Gasps flooded the room, and I wasn't sure if it was a reaction to my tone of voice or the fact I said the work *magic* when I was on trial for helping a magical being escape.

I clenched my fist so hard that my nails dug into my skin, but I showed no sign on my face that I had made a mistake.

I was not guilty, not of *that* at least. I would not act like I was.

"Lies," He spat. He then reached for an item across from him on his desk. "Recognize this?" he asked, holding up a hairpin.

I squinted my eyes and dread filled my bones as I recognized the hairpin.

The tip was small, but the back of it was just large enough to have three initials engraved on the bottom.

My whole body froze and I could feel the heat rise to my neck. I had been wearing that pin when I was in that cell, and when I was released. It couldn't be mine…

I anxiously felt the back of my hair as I held on to the shred of hope that it wasn't *my* pin that he was holding.

All hope was lost as I felt the smooth surface of my hair.

No pin.

As I was walking out with the guards, the prisoner must have snatched it and used it to pick the lock on the cell door.

"I did not give that to him," I stated plainly. My face showed no signs of nerves, even though inside I was feeling quite the opposite. My heart was practically in my throat.

"So, you recognize this to be yours then, Amara?" He said my name like it was poison on his tongue. The audience gasped again and I could hear Poppy let out a stifled sob.

I wouldn't look. I *couldn't* look.

I didn't want that to be my last image of her if those were my last moments there. "Yes. It's mine, but I did not give that to him, it must have fallen out, or he could have stolen it from my hair," I replied.

"Very well." He clicked his tongue and finger brushed his short beard that swallowed his chin. "Because of your crimes and the fact you will not admit to them… I sentence you to banishment, to live out the rest of your days above."

He smacked a gavel onto the wooden stand. "What a shame it is. You would've made such—" His eyes roamed down my body and stopped at my hips. "—*Great* offspring for my Mason. Too bad you turned out to be an insubordinate woman."

I kept my face stoic even though I was sneering on the inside.

"You all are dismissed." He raised his voice to the small crowd gathered behind me.

My body went numb, but I refused to cry. I wasn't going to beg for pity when I hadn't done anything wrong.

Maybe my pride would be the death of me, but without it, I was no one. I was not going to balk and own up to something that I had not done.

Even if it meant being banished. It didn't matter anyway. Whether I owned up to it or not, once someone is brought to that room, their future is set in stone. I knew exactly what my fate was the second I stepped in there.

Banishment would have been my punishment whether I admitted to it or continued telling the truth.

So, I would go out honest.

I didn't look at anyone that I knew as the guards walked me out, I couldn't bear to see the looks on their faces even though I could imagine them in my head.

Everything inside of me begged to give one last look to Poppy. I felt her gaze on me as I was led past her. I just couldn't do it.

I didn't want to remember her that way. Sobbing and heartbroken.

No, I would remember her always cheerful self. The way she called me out when I was being dramatic or overthinking. She always brought me back down to earth when my mind was in the clouds.

That's what I would remember.

I didn't have to look at her to know that she was a mess. I heard the sniffles and the almost silent cry that she let out as I passed by.

Even if I didn't hear anything, I knew our lifetime of friendship would call for a heart-wrenching reaction. One that I just couldn't face.

Because if I did, I wasn't sure I would be able to get that image out of my mind. It would replay over and over again. Forever.

I also knew I would break down right then in there, and I wouldn't give Alastor that satisfaction.

As much as it pained me not to say a real goodbye to her, we already said our goodbyes.

I wasn't sure how my father reacted, but I wasn't going to look at him either. Not because I was sad, but because I just did not care to see his reaction.

It had always felt like I was his means to an end. If he was crying, it was probably because now he had no one to carry on his legacy, and not because he was losing his daughter.

The fact my mother did not even bother to show up said enough about how she felt. My eyes burned at the sudden realization of just how little my parents cared for me. And how Poppy had shown more feelings for me than my parents.

She was my true family.

The guards led me up the spiral staircase that seemed to never end. I was panting only halfway through the climb and the guard holding my wrists behind my back snickered at me.

"I bet you she won't last a day up there," he joked to the other guard.

I felt my skin turn molten at his downright evil remark. He was laughing at me because he knew that I was going to die.

Disgusting.

The other guard bit back a laugh as he responded. "A day? Try two hours!"

The two guards howled and I took a deep breath to steady myself. I had been so close to shouting back at them and asking how they could be so cruel. How they could laugh at someone's downfall. Innocent or not.

I knew it wouldn't help my case though. If I did that, they would most likely kill me on the spot and claim that I was being *"unruly."*

So I listened.

I listened to them make fun of me for being helpless.

For being a *woman*.

"Should we have some fun with her before we send her out?" the first guard asked the other one.

Every nerve in my body stilled as his words sunk deep into a heaviness in my chest.

The first guard practically undressed me with his eyes and then his friend responded. "No. Alastor said to banish her. As much as I would *love* to defile this flower, he didn't say this one was up for grabs."

Up for grabs?

As if I was an extra helping of potatoes at dinner time that was left unclaimed.

Sickness swirled in my stomach. They would have to kill me first.

The fact that they had probably been allowed to do this before to other women made my stomach churn. Anger seemed to burn holes through my clenched fists.

"Fine," the first guard huffed.

I knew that we had reached the top of the stairwell when we got to a large door with an iron bar stretched across to keep it locked. One of the guards pulled the bar to the side and then the heavy metal door creaked open.

When it was wide enough for my body to clear it, he used all of his force to throw me through the door, and I fell face flat on the prickly ground.

The sting from the rays of the sun burned as they met my skin. It felt like I was being rubbed over and over again with sandpaper.

I couldn't see.

Everywhere I looked I only saw bright white light. I couldn't hear past the ring in my ears and my heart thumped against my chest so hard it almost felt like everything else had slowed.

I closed my eyes as hard as I could until the ringing stopped and my eyes adjusted to the sunlight.

I had never seen the sun before, part of me did not even think it existed. It started to seem like a myth or something out of a fairytale. The existence of the sun was something I began to question even though I *knew* it was needed to grow our food. Even though I knew the sun technically *existed*, it didn't exist to me. Not in my reality.

I never knew what the absence of darkness looked like, and not just a few candles providing a bubble of light in a pitch-black room. I had never seen true, real, natural, light. After a few minutes, I peeked through my eyelids, my eyes still stinging and burning from the rays of the sun, but they had adjusted enough to where I could vaguely make out what was around me.

As my vision returned, I looked down at my pale skin and never realized how truly colorless it was in the underground. Where there was no light and no other colors besides beige to compare my skin to. I opened my eyes wide and looked all around, spinning in circles to take in everything.

A cold stream fell down my cheek. I wiped it away just for another one to roll down in its wake.

For a moment, all the fear that I felt, all of the uncertainty, floated away as if it were ash in the wind.

It was beautiful.

PART TWO

A Kingdom of Light

8

I stood outside of the closed gate taking in everything. Every sound, color, smell, and feeling. I heard leaves rustling, bees buzzing, and the howl of the cool wind caressing my hair and skin. I felt its cool touch on my body drying up any beads of sweat that had formed.

The natural aromas of the plants gave off scents that were like nothing I smelled before underground. Until that moment, I had only experienced the natural scents of damp stone and smoke from the torches. The plants gave off scents that were similar to the roses in my room, but much more intense.

Then, there were the colors. There were *so* many colors. The greens were everywhere, on the leaves of the trees, stems of flowers, blades of grass, all a different shade that seemed to swirl and blend into a perfect painting. Pinks, reds, blues, and purples are pasted on the flowers. The sky was a perfect shade of baby blue with soft white clumps of cloud scattering throughout.

I knew all of those colors because we learned them in school in the underground. They would show us a piece of paper with different colors painted on it, but I never thought I would see them in such a natural state.

As I took everything in, I felt a pang of emotions hit my chest.

I felt angry—*angry* that this had been hidden from me all those years. Then as soon as the anger hit, so did the fear.

I'm alone. Truly alone.

I had nowhere to go, and no weapons, food, or knowledge of the world.

My breaths started to quicken and become shorter and shorter than the last. I looked around, my head spinning.

I caught a glimpse of an enclosed garden near the gate to the underground. The fence was high enough to where I needed to be four times as high to jump over it.

My eyes then stopped on a path in front of me and my feet began trampling down it before my mind had fully caught up.

I was adrift, my destination uncertain, but the need to seek sanctuary, to conceal myself away from whatever creatures lurked, consumed me.

The unknown beasts that prowled the wilds of the land above, *the land I was now stuck on,* were a mystery to me, and one that I was in no hurry to solve.

Just then, I remembered the name of the lost, forgotten, abandoned land of the humans and from a book I found in the library once. It was titled, "Histories of Nymyria."

I had brought it back to our dwelling and my mother told me it was never to be spoken of again before she threw the book into the fire.

I hadn't thought the name of much importance and wondered why it was forbidden to speak.

It must have been what the land was called, and why she told me never to say it again.

"*Nymyria,*" I scoffed to myself.

The land where humans used to dwell. Before everything was destroyed.

Even the name of these lands sounded magical, like something out of a fairytale. That's how it felt all those years to learn about the world above.

The dangerous world where creatures run rampant. It was why we had to move underground in the first place.

This place felt like a story that was told to children to keep their imaginations active. Now, I was living in it.

The land was so amazing I could hardly describe its beauty in words. It didn't seem threatening or evil, but I hadn't explored much of it either.

No matter how beautiful it was, I had to find a shelter or at least a place to hide before I was found.

My feet pounded against the ground, my heart racing as I fled. I was determined to put as much distance between myself and the lurking terrors as I could, wherever they were.

I kicked mud up behind myself as my feet skipped over each other in a perfect rhythm before they came to a sudden halt and my entire body tensed.

I could make out the silhouette of what looked to be a person, someone in a long black cloak with a hood covering their head.

I took refuge behind a tree and as I focused on steadying the rise and fall of my chest, I willed my breathing to slow in case they could hear my exhaustion.

Maybe it was a human? It is possible they were a banished one. Maybe they could help me?

I crept around and peeked behind the tree hesitantly to see that the figure was gone.

I quickly whipped my head back around and it felt as if my lungs had deflated as the mass of black and withered white skin was now standing an inch from my face.

I let out a high-pitched shriek as I stared at the decayed-looking human with hallowed out pits where eyeballs should have been.

Its wrinkled, almost rotten, skin and bony figure made it appear as if it was dead. Soulless.

It was human in its likeness, but it was as if all life was drained out from it.

The creature's gaping mouth opened wide, revealing a pale, veiny tongue that slithered toward me with sickening speed.

I backed up into a tree and the creature lunged forward, locking me in.

Before I could react, its tongue latched onto my cheek, its touch like a thousand needles piercing into me. With another burst of movement, it hurled forward and sank its teeth into my cheek, drawing forth a flow of blood.

I fought with all my might, pushing and pulling, struggling to break free of its deadly embrace, but it was no use. I kicked and screamed out for help even though I knew no one was there. No one would help me.

My strength was fading away, the weakness seeping in as my head spun and my eyes grew heavy with the weight of my waning consciousness.

I am going to die.

My breaths shortened and I looked around in panic trying to find anything that could help me.

There was nothing I could use as a weapon. Only tree branches, but they were far too high to grab a hold of.

The trees started to look like a blurry smear of green and brown paint as I began to fade.

No. Not like this.

As a last-ditch effort, I reached my arm up and clenched it around its engorged neck so that my blood flowed down.

It let out an ear-piercing shriek and unlatched its teeth from my cheek. I then strangled its revolting tongue with my other hand, the small, needled points on it rooting themselves into my skin.

I didn't care.

The creature was screaming out in pain, and I only clenched harder.

Then its empty eyes met mine, and I felt my energy deplete. As if it was now draining my life source instead of my blood.

I began to accept my fate, knowing there was nothing else I could do against it.

Then, before I could blink the creature was knocked back twenty paces from where I stood, pinning it against a tree.

A warm, strong grip closed around my shoulder, pulling me back with unexpected force.

Suddenly, time seemed to stretch out before me, elongating each passing moment until a single second felt like an eternity.

I had no concept of what was happening.

And then, before I knew it, I was in the air.

I felt as if I was doing somersaults the way my stomach leaped into my throat.

Strong arms gripped me from behind as I *flew* through the sky.

I was heaving to get air into my lungs, each breath felt like it was not enough as I worked to calm myself down.

"Put me down!" I screamed to the figure gripping me. A strong form was pressed up against me, but I was being held too tight to look back and see who held me.

For all I knew, it could be another one of those creatures carrying me to its nest.

Higher we flew into the low-hanging clouds.

"I could let you go, but I don't think you would like that very much," a familiar voice shouted from behind me and then chuckled.

As much as I wanted to kick against the person and fight to be let go, I knew it was better I stay still than to drop to my death.

Clouds surrounded us and light danced through the small water droplets that formed them.

Yellow and pink light shined through the clouds, illuminating everything in a dreamy haze.

I hated that it was yet another beautiful sight.

Before I could convince myself not to, my arm was reaching out and touching the clouds. I swirled my hand through one in an attempt to grab the droplets.

My hands became covered in wet mist as the cloud dissipated.

Remembering that a stranger held me, I shouted back, "Who are you and where are we going?" The strong wind blew my hair into my mouth as I tried to speak.

"Somewhere safe," was all I heard.

The voice was so familiar, but I didn't even bother trying to place where I had heard it before since I had only ever been underground and it couldn't possibly have been any of the people I knew.

We started to make our descent, and once the tip of my feet touched the ground, I shoved off of the stranger and charged forward a few steps when I noticed how different everything seemed.

The air was clearer, the colors of the plants and trees were more vivid, and the scents were much stronger.

Shimmering particles danced and sparkled all around me, each movement slow and deliberate like they had a mind of their own. I reached out to grab one, but they were so tiny I could barely see it on my hand.

A honeyed voice sliced through the stillness of the forest, causing me to jump in surprise. "It's alright. You're safe now."

I whirled around, remembering I still needed to find out who or what was flying me through the air.

Slowly, I turned to face the source of the voice, my eyes widening as they landed on the tall man with golden eyes and silver iridescent hair that seemed to glow at different angles as if it had absorbed sunlight itself. Even the perimeter of his body shined bright.

It was the same stranger I had encountered just the day before in the prison, and yet, there was something different about him now.

As my eyes glided along his body, studying him, I realized he had… *wings*.

He hadn't had them in the prison. As I looked closer I realized they were made of vines of ivy. Just then, they retracted back and the vines pulled back into his wrists.

I gasped and then jumped backward, almost tripping over myself. Choking on the air, I managed to breathe a single word, "How?"

He ignored my question as if there had been an obvious answer. A sense of danger and warning emanated from him, reminding me that I had trespassed into forbidden territory.

"What are you doing out here?" he demanded.

I stood for a minute in silence, processing what had just happened to me. Finally, I managed to speak, my voice barely above a whisper. "I was banished," I admitted, the weight of those three simple words heavy on my tongue. Not that he would even understand the human system, but it was all I could think of to say.

"You almost died," he said as if that wasn't obvious. "You should be more careful."

"Yes, because it was my choice to almost die due to that creature," I snapped. "Where are we?" I frantically looked around, my heart slowing as I calmed down. I knew we were somewhere different than before. Everything just seemed *brighter*.

"The Light Kingdom." I must have looked utterly perplexed because he continued "There is a veil around the kingdom to keep us safe from the soul reapers."

"' The soul reapers?'" I muttered.

"They can drain your soul," he said so calmly I could feel my breakfast coming up. "They are nasty little things, but easy enough for *us* to avoid."

Us. He means… whatever *he* is. Not human, but…

I jolted backward and fell back with my arms to grasp the tree behind me leaning my body weight into it. "What... what are you then? Do you drain human souls too?" I quivered.

He let out a faint chuckle and his eyes met mine. "No. We are quite the opposite. We are the fates."

9

"*The fates.*"

He had said those two words as if they were so simple, simple enough to where I wouldn't need an explanation.

I knew their names were never to be spoken, just like the name of the land.

The name was so unfamiliar to me, and yet it was as if I had known it all along. Known it well enough that it sent a shiver down my spine as the words slipped from his mouth.

I surveyed his body starting from the tip of his head and making my way down from there. His short, tousled, silver hair gleamed. It was then that I noticed his ears were pointed at the top ever so slightly, and his skin shined with a warm summer glow.

It was as if the sun had been absorbed by the perimeters of his body. His skin was so soft, supple, and bright. Never had I seen skin so beautiful.

He was tan too. A quality no one underground possessed. I made it to his waist when I jolted out of my gaze and dragged my eyes back to meet his. By the expression on his face, he knew I had been scanning him, but he hadn't commented on it.

"Your ears, the glow around you, I don't understand," I said, my voice wavering.

"I am a fate." His eyes met the ground and he gripped the blade on his thigh. "As I'm sure you know, we have magic…" Sun rays peered through the trees and danced on his iridescent hair.

I gulped as he continued.

"It either comes from all things light, that being the sun, or from darkness. Since there are only two sources of our power, we are split into two kingdoms: light fates and dark fates. The light ones, which I am—" He paused to wink at me. "—Are mostly good. We have a sort of lightness in our hearts, in our spirits, that guides our choices and who we are. The dark fates on the other hand are mostly…"

"Not good?" I cut him off, wanting him to speak faster.

"Yes, you could say that," he sighed with what seemed to be distress.

It was obvious there was something about my statement that bothered him, but I wouldn't push him on it. Not now at least. He was telling me all this, the least I could do was not push.

Why *was* he telling me all this?

"The darkness can consume them if they choose it. Many dark fates that have gone through traumatic or emotionally exhausting experiences can allow the darkness to fester and grow within themselves, not allowing any room for love, kindness, or… light. Those fates are the ones you have to be careful of. Hence why we are called the fates. It is up to fate to decide what each of us will be." His eyes grew weary as he finished speaking. I could see there was a history behind his words that irked him.

His words seemed familiar, from a memory I couldn't quite place. For some reason, I had an intense desire to change the conversation.

"Why are you telling me this?" I breathed as I attempted to grasp the information he was providing me. It was all too much.

"Because then you can decide for yourself."

"Decide what? Do you think telling me all this will change my mind about you? About *your* kind?"

He recoiled at my words and then sighed.

"Thanks for this *enlightening* encounter and for saving me from the soul reaper, but I have to be going now," I said as I marched away from him.

"Where are you going to go?" He followed my steps and I could feel his looming presence behind me.

"Don't know," I admitted. "But somewhere away from you."

"It's not safe out here. Not for a human at least. The veil protects us from those creatures, but it won't protect you from—"

"From you? From your kind?" I spun around and crossed my arms.

He sighed and looked around to deflect. "Look, as good as *we* are, many of us will see a human and be scared. They wouldn't know what to do, so yes that puts you in danger. But not because we want to hurt you—"

"Scared?" I scoffed. "Of me? That's ridiculous! We are the ones who are scared of *you*."

"You may not trust me, and I understand that, but it's not like where you used to live. You will not survive a day out in the wilds of Nymyria. Not when you have spent your whole life underground."

Used to live. Those words seem to strike my heart as if it were a dagger twisting in all directions.

"And beyond the veil, it's especially unsafe. It's overridden with reapers who would love nothing more to destroy my race, and yours. The veil has kept our kingdom safe while those soulless creatures roam the other side of the veil... even us fates are too scared to be on the other side for too long, just think of what they would do to a human girl—"

"'Human girl.' Unbelievable." My stomach twisted into knots and heat swirled in my chest. "And you mean to tell me that you *fates* have been sitting here happy and safe from these creatures, while mortals were forced, driven underground to live?" The heat rose in my face and my cheeks became crimson.

Oh god, I just yelled at a man—a fate.

I couldn't stop myself.

"While you all have been up here, we have been living in fear for almost a century!" I screamed taking steps towards him and blocking him against a tree. "Most of us don't even know what the world truly looks like. Never have seen the sun. Or even picture what a world could look like beyond stone walls, darkness, and fire." My face grew solemn.

"We tried," he softly muttered. "We tried to convince your leader at the time to move with us, over the veil, but he refused. He said he didn't want help from evil creatures like us. We presume he thought it was a trap to take over his people. He would rather force his whole mortal continent underground than live in harmony with the fates."

His eyes grew wide as he let out a sigh. "His pride wouldn't let him admit that he couldn't save his people, not without our magic. So, he made a new civilization underground. People were mad at first, so I heard, but after a century when the old generation who had lived through being taken underground had passed over, the newer generations didn't know anything different. Less of a fight. Even the leader, his son grew up to know nothing different, and same with his son after that." Something like regret seemed to sweep over his eyes.

As much as I hated it, a feeling deep down inside had wanted to believe him. His words were so sincere, and his eyes. He had so much emotion, so many memories he had recalled behind those eyes as if he truly wanted to save them, *us*.

"What's your name?" I ordered as I stepped back from him. I didn't want to talk about it anymore. I knew what happened in the past wasn't directly *his* fault, but his kind—they could have done something more to help. Either way, I wasn't just going to automatically believe him. Not after everything I had been taught. Not when my ancestor had been killed by one. And especially not when he possesses magic. He could have been using it to trick me.

"Arryn," he said with a sense of relief that I changed the topic once again.

"Amara."

"I know." He smiled and tapped his wrists to jog my memory of the cuffs that had once been on his wrists and to remind me of the night we had been in the jail together.

Just then my face twisted into a grimace as I pounced over to him, backing him against a tree.

"You—" my face heated while heat rose in my chest as I remembered the whole reason I was there in the first place. "You stole my hairpin, you unlocked your cuffs, and—and you're the reason I was exiled!" I pointed into his face.

"I'm sorry," was all he could muster up. His words convey the exact opposite of his face. He wasn't even going to try and deny it? For some reason, his honesty angered me even more.

"You're sorry? I have nothing because of you. I have nowhere to go, no food, nothing to protect myself with, no home." My voice cracked and my eyes began to burn. "I don't know what to do." I slowly turned to blink away the water welling up in my eyes.

What a mess I was. I couldn't help it though. I had been through so much in the past few hours it was hard to accept that any of it was real.

Arryn's face dimmed and the glow around him seemed to fade. "Come with me." Was all he said before he grabbed my hand and wind flew through my hair. I let out a high-pitched shriek as a small sapling beneath us grew tall and wrapped around our bodies as it grew. In a matter of seconds, we could touch the clouds.

We zoomed through the sky and landed in front of a beautiful home resting on a grassy cliff just a few moments later with a porch stretching across the whole front side. The tree grew backward, retracting to where we had initially been.

"What was that?" I struggled to catch my breath, once again pushing out of his arms that were tightened around me.

It all happened so fast that I didn't even realize I had been *in the sky*. Again.

"Magic." He flashed a cheeky smile.

There were trees of all different colors surrounding the perimeter of the home and a rose garden in front.

"You can." I breathed deeply trying to get as much oxygen as possible before I passed out from shock. "You can… grow… plants? To *fly*?" I questioned as my face contorted into confusion.

"Yes," he said as if it had been idiotic to ask such a thing. "I can make them take other forms, bend them to my will… of course, I can't actually *fly*, but I can use plants to make it seem that way."

"Right. That… makes sense."

It did not make sense, but it's not like any of this made *any* sense.

"Those can make you fly?" I pointed to the ivy vines on each of his wrists.

He ran a hand through his silver strands. "Ah, so you noticed the wings before," he chuckled as his vines began to travel up his arms and to his back. They curled up and out, then downward to form large wing shapes. The leaves on the ivy then began to grow and stretch across the vines to close off the middle.

"I am indeed a light fate, but my special magic is plants. Every one of us has a specialty magic of some sort. Some can control the weather, some can speak to animals, my best friend can turn people to stone, and mine... is plants."

"...Plants?" I asked sarcastically. "Your unique gift is gardening?" I joked, even though I knew what he could do. His magic was much more than that, but I was not going to act amazed.

His gaze locked onto me, a blank canvas for his emotions until a symphony of laughter erupted from him. Laughter cascaded from his lips, causing his head to tilt skyward, and his hand clutched his stomach.

I wasn't sure what to do in that moment. Was I supposed to laugh with him? Was I allowed to?

"You're funny," he said finally coming down from his amusement as he let out a straggled cough.

For a few moments, I waited for a specific phrase to slip out from him before I responded.

For a woman.

But it never came.

"Thank you," I said reluctantly and looked to the ground, not quite sure where to look or where to put my hands.

"I can grow plants and change their forms. It is also common for some fates to also have some sort of shape-shifting ability. Mine is within the plants that I grow. So not only can I grow them…" he said stretching out his wrist. "…but I can form them into whatever I want and do whatever I want. It would be easier if I just showed you—"

"No!" I shouted before he lifted his hand to do whatever he was about to do. "I don't want to see," I spat. "I don't care. I saw enough."

I was not going to befriend a fate, let alone show interest in their magic that has caused humans so much harm. Admittedly I was curious, hence all the questions, but I couldn't continue.

He nodded quietly as he brought his arm back to his side. "Well, if you ever want to see—"

"I won't." I cut him off not bothering to care what the consequences were. I didn't care that I was a woman and that he was a man—a *fate*.

Whatever trouble I would get in for speaking to him that way, I would deal with it.

"You can stay here." He changed the subject as he outstretched his arm towards the house we landed in front of. "It's the least I can do."

I had not even processed what he had just said because my mind was still racing trying to make sense of everything he just did and told me.

Just then, my attention then became fixated on what stood before me. A large white home with gold flecks shimmering as the sun reflected off of them.

"How?" I asked as I couldn't seem to look away from the floating lights.

He didn't say anything as he waved his hand in front of me and flecks of sun began falling from it, as if *that* was supposed to answer my question. *Magic.*

I dropped to my knees partly in awe of the beautiful home, and partly because the painful realization had hit me just then.

My life as I knew it was over.

That girl from the underground, she was gone.

10

As I stood before the ivory house that was taller than any of the trees around us, my gaze swept over its majestic form in absolute awe.

Four pillars adorned the front, stretching along the length of the porch. The front door was a large arched gate with golden bars in front of it. On top of the house, a series of cone-shaped peaks jutted out, each one crowned with a panel of arched stained glass windows.

House was an understatement for what it was. A mansion was a more fitting word.

Maybe even castle.

The castle rested atop a grassy hill. The tips of the castle seemed to reach into the clouds with golden sunlight shining through.

But it was the rose garden that laid in front of the castle that truly captured my attention. My feet moved of their own accord, leading me towards the row of deep red blooms that stood at attention like soldiers, all at the same height as if they had been meticulously trained. Each petal was a vibrant hue. The deep red color looked like it had been brushed on with the finest of paints.

I gazed at the beautiful flowers and my eyes began to sting as I remembered a memory from my birthday a year ago. I learned what roses were in class that day when our teacher gave a lesson about plants. She had mentioned roses in passing when explaining the different herbs and teas that we drink. In that moment it had occurred to me that I shared a middle name with such a flower.

A flower I had not been able to see. Curiosity struck me, and I needed to know what they looked like, how they felt, and *smelled*. I raced back to my dwelling to beg my mother for a single rose. I knew it would be difficult for her to get one, but not impossible. Certain people in the underground were allowed to go above to farm the land, in a contained safe greenhouse of course, that she could ask. I had never implored my parents for anything.

Even when my clothes didn't fit me anymore, I wouldn't ask them for new ones. I never wanted to be a burden or trouble them. But that day, when I learned about roses, I had never desired anything more in my entire life. I would've given anything to see one. To smell one. I yearned to hold one in my hands and to feel the supple petals upon my fingertips.

The longing was so intense within me that it felt as if a silent request had been sent out into the world. And as if in response, a warm sensation bloomed within my chest, a sign that my wish was heard.

I still remember the expression on my mother's face when I asked her. She tried to hide it, but I could see the disappointment in her eyes, not with me, but with herself. The fact she couldn't get them for me. Or maybe it wasn't the pain of her not being able to provide one for me, but the pain that I had even asked for such a thing. Looking back on it, it was not common to request items from above. It was frowned upon actually.

When I saw the pain seep into her face, I changed the subject and accepted that I would not be getting a rose then or probably ever.

The very next day, I had come home from class, and to my surprise, my whole room was filled with red roses. The color red was plastered on every surface. It was the first time I had truly cried. Sobbed. But not because I was sad, but because I had never been so happy in my entire existence. My mother seemed to not know what I was talking about when I thanked her profusely, and she ignored the roses in my room. Never acknowledged them. But I was grateful. Somehow those roses never died. Still fresh up to the day I was banished from the underground. I had wondered many times if my mother had replaced them with fresh ones every week since my birthday last year. After she refused to acknowledge them, I decided it was better not to ask in case it would get her in trouble.

It was the only thing she had ever done that made me feel like she loved me.

I jolted back into the present as I reached out to touch one of the roses and then pulled my hand back quickly. I assumed he wouldn't want me messing with the *perfect* garden outside of his *perfect* castle.

"You can have one if you like." I heard Arryn stalking behind me.

My eyes widened and I turned to face him. "I wouldn't want to ruin the perfect garden you have here. One missing would be an eye sore." I snapped.

With measured steps he advanced toward the garden, his gaze trained on the rose I had been eyeing. He extended his hand to it and gracefully plucked it from its stem.

He then reached for my hands and before I could object, he pulled them to his chest and unfolded my fingers as he gently placed the rose in the middle of my palms. His soft hands trailed down my fingers before he pulled them away.

My chest began to warm and I averted my gaze, fearful that tears might spill from my eyes again as they did when I found the roses in my bedroom.

Do not cry.

"You may take as many as you like." He smiled and made his way to the front gate of the castle. "Come on, let me show you where you will be staying."

As much as I wanted to throw the rose in his face and tell him I didn't need his help, I couldn't fight the wave of relief that coursed through me at his words. Calming the restless beating of my heart, and absolving the fear of spending the night in the unforgiving wilderness.

I plucked a single petal from the rose in my hands and let it fall to the ground before I wiped away a stray tear that fell down my cheek.

I couldn't fathom why he was extending his kindness towards me after how rude I was to him, or why he had come to my rescue when the jaws of the soul reaper were moments away from claiming me. Fates don't help humans.

How was it that he was even there at the exact moment I was banished?

But before these thoughts could settle in my mind, they dissipated, and I found myself trailing behind him, clutching the rose in my hands, as he led the way into the castle.

✥ ✥ ✥

I trailed behind Arryn as he led me through the hallways. The walls were covered in white wallpaper with gold swirling patterns that resembled ivy vines with paintings hanging neatly and evenly spaced. There were sculptures and expensive-looking vases, chalices, and jewels on display. The ceilings were arched with golden trim and white columns that went from the top to the floor.

He made his way to the grand staircase and led me up to the second level.

Gold chandeliers hung from the ceilings with candles placed on each post. Shiny prisms dangled from the body and captured the sunlight that showed through the stained glass windows.

"This can be your room." Arryn extended his arm out to lead me into the large room with tall windows that opened up to a balcony. The room seemed to be an office as there was a desk and a large bookshelf against the wall. I spun in a circle wondering where I was going to sleep and he must have read my thoughts because I blinked and then the desk was replaced with a bed draped with soft pink velvet.

"I figured a bed would be more comfortable than a desk." He flashed me a sheepish grin as he nervously scratched the back of his head.

My eyes darted to meet his as I tried to form words but they wouldn't come out. All I could muster up was a measly, "Thank you."

He nodded and then made his way to the door to exit. Before his hand made contact with the door handle I impulsively told him to wait. His head turned to face mine but his body still faced the door. "Why?" I asked in a soft but stern tone.

"Why, what?" he shot back.

"Why are you doing this? Why are you giving me a place to live in your house? You said that you wouldn't feel right leaving me in the woods because it was your fault that I was banished but..."

I crossed my arms and looked around the lavish room with gold drapes covering the windows and gold embellishments all around the white wooden bed frame. "This—this isn't what you do for someone just because you simply *feel bad*. Especially since I have made it pretty clear that I am not fond of you, and probably never will be. Why help someone like me?"

As soon as those last two words slipped out, I could see the mood shift within him. His back stiffened and his warm face faded to a cold expressionless mask. "I just have to. It is the right thing to do." Before I could say another word, he opened the door and shut it behind him.

I just have to. His words echoed in my mind for a few moments before I shrugged and made my way to the bookshelf. If he wanted to help me I wasn't going to reject it. I didn't trust him, but I couldn't deny the fact that this was a place to stay. And a nice one at that. It was better than sleeping in the woods.

It was *a lot* better than sleeping in the woods.

Just because he was helping me though, did not mean I was going to just immediately forget what he was.

❀ ❀ ❀

After a few hours of looking through the books on the shelf and exploring my new bedroom, I heard a faint knock on the door. I hesitated but then slowly made my way to touch the knob.

Before I could open it, the door swung open colliding full force with my forehead. "What the-!" I yelped.

"Oh! By the Threads of Fate, I am so sorry!" a comforting female voice replied. I rubbed my head for a few moments and then looked up to see a short woman around what seemed to be my age with golden, honey-blonde hair and freckles that painted her face like stars in the sky. Her skin was tan, and a few shades darker than Arryn's.

I wasn't sure that I had ever seen a woman as beautiful as her. Her skin glowed and her hair shined like there were strands of sunlight spread throughout. It seemed as if golden tinsel was sewn into her hair.

"Here." She extended her empty hand to my forehead and a sack of ice appeared in it, pressing to the purple lump already forming.

"Thanks," I replied hoarsely and placed my hand over the bag.

"I was coming to introduce myself to you, and also get you for dinner. That clearly went well." She chuckled nervously. "I'm Caris."

"Amara," I winced.

"Yeah, I know." She smiled brightly. Her teeth were so white I could've sworn they sparkled.

"Arryn told me what he has—his mistake," she corrected herself. "I can't believe he's the reason for your banishment. I'm so sorry, he can be such an airhead sometimes," she said as she lightly hit the top of her head with her palm.

"Right," I groaned as I adjusted the ice bag on my face to the colder side.

"Well," she opened the door once more and looked at me as if she was waiting for me to follow "Dinner is ready. I hope you like venison!" Her lips curved into a radiant smile, a glow so befitting of a light fate that even her eyes joined in, twinkling with joy.

11

I did *not* like venison. We did not have much meat in the underground because it was too difficult to hunt for animals. It had been a lot easier to grow vegetables and fruits safely because it could be done in a contained area. Only a few of the most trusted helpers were allowed to farm and hunt, so food in general was fairly scarce. Hunting required our people to venture out into the forest above. Occasionally we would feast on rabbits, squirrels, and sometimes various birds. Whenever a deer was killed, and it was not often, it usually went to Alastor and his family.

I shifted the venison from one side of my plate to the other with my fork over and over again until dinner was over. Arryn had sat on one side with Caris and I sat on the other.

They talked very softly and mentioned to each other some cryptic "plans" that they were to fulfill, but I was too in my head to truly hear a word they were saying.

Physically, and mentally, I was still in shock from being banished. I was expecting to break down at any moment, but it hadn't happened yet.

I was sad, but I still hadn't had that moment of realization yet where the emotions hit me all at once. I barely even cried, but I had been so busy since I was banished that I hadn't even had time to think about what I just went through. What it would mean for my life and my future. I figured the sadness hadn't really hit me yet and that it would probably sweep over me at the least expected time.

Just then a few housemaids rushed in, taking the empty plates from the center of the table and replacing them with sweets.

It was strange to see maids who looked so happy. They were dressed in bright gold and smiled as if it was their greatest pleasure to serve us.

"Amara?" Caris said loudly.

My head shot up and I stepped out of my thoughts. "Yes?"

"I asked if you wanted something else to eat?" Her smile enveloped me in a warm embrace, instantly putting me at ease. "It's okay if you don't like it, it's a bit of an acquired taste."

"No, no. Dinner is great," I lied and mustered up a faint smile. No matter how kind she seemed to be, I did not want to take the chance of upsetting a fate. "I am just not that hungry… after everything."

Arryn and Caris's eyes met and they frowned at each other before both looking back towards me.

It was strange to see such a bland expression on their bright faces.

"Of course," Caris replied. "Maybe you should just go get some rest. We have a big day tomorrow."

"What?" My brows lowered and I set my fork down.

"I am going to show you around! Take you to all my favorite spots. I figured you would want to see it all after being underground so long—" Before Caris could finish her sentence, Arryn cut her off by clearing his throat.

"Thanks for joining us for dinner Amara. You are free to do whatever you like. If you don't feel up for it tomorrow, you don't have to go." Arryn bowed his head as if excusing me from the table.

My heart warmed and for the first time, I felt like I had a choice.

Granted I didn't really have one, as I had nowhere else to go. Staying there was my only choice.

Regardless of what I felt obligated to do, Arryn's words did not make me feel that way.

Nothing was left up to me underground. Even the food I ate was chosen for me.

"Thank you." I made long eye contact with Arryn and then flashed a fake smile as I rose from my chair and pushed it into the table. If anything I would pretend to be grateful so that I wouldn't upset two fates.

His lips curled upward and then he drifted his eyes south, scanning my chest. I had a white blouse on that I found in the closet of my bedroom. I looked down to where his eyes were directed and I saw that it had been completely see-through.

Shit, shit, shit!

As if sensing my discomfort, he averted his gaze back towards my eyes and acted like my shirt wasn't as thin as morning mist.

That small act of courtesy I was very grateful for.

Heat immediately spread to my cheeks in embarrassment and I hugged my arms around my chest. "Thank you for the offer Caris, I will let you know in the morning."

Her eyes lit up and then she nodded as I ran out of the dining room, making my way back to my new bedroom.

❦ ❦ ❦

I was so exhausted when I got back to my room.

Mentally more so than physically.

I couldn't stop the thoughts from whirling in my head all night. The conflicting feelings that I felt. As much as I wanted to hate Arryn and Caris, I couldn't ignore the fact that they had been so nice to me. Aside from Arryn's mistake of getting me banished, which would take a lot of time for me to get over, they seemed… *decent.*

Especially Caris. She was practically light incarnate. Something told me she would never be caught without a smile on her face. I couldn't imagine what she would even look like with a frown. For some reason, I hoped that I would never see it either.

I plopped onto the velvet bed and closed my eyes. As much as I wished to drift into a deep sleep, my thoughts swirled and I knew I wouldn't be able to quiet them. Not tonight.

I grabbed the book I had been eyeing earlier titled *Fated*. The book had a black cloth hardcover with gold swirls around the edges and the binding. The title also shimmered in gold. The book felt nice in my hands. It was heavy and the cloth cover added a nice texture that was satisfying to hold. I figured that if a book possessed such aesthetic and tactile appeal, surely it held promise as a captivating read. Laying my head back down on the bed, I opened the book and began to read.

❁ ❁ ❁

My gaze widened, and an involuntary gasp somehow escaped from my lips, as I delved deeper into chapter twenty-three of the book. It had been a few hours since I first picked up the book. A rush of adrenaline coursed through my veins, setting my heart at a pace twice as fast as usual.

At long last, the protagonist and the love interest had succumbed to the undeniable attraction that had simmered beneath the surface for countless chapters.

But it wasn't the tension between them that made it like nothing else I have ever read. No, it was the fact that two people loved each other enough to let the world burn around them as long as they could be together.

What a story.

It was a beautiful tapestry woven from someone's imagination. I couldn't even fathom how someone could come up with something so enchanting.

I also couldn't believe that I had no idea that this existed. There were no stories of love underground. The only books to read were those for educational purposes and books about the history of our people.

There was one book of fairytales, but I hardly remembered it since it had disappeared when I was a young child.

Nevertheless, I always enjoyed reading. It helped me relax, and jumping into a book was easier than facing the constant thoughts that plagued my brain. It was always an escape for me. A way to escape my life and my mind.

A flush of warmth spread across my cheeks as I continued to immerse myself in the captivating scene—meticulously drawn out, revealing every nuance in explicit detail. It was not solely the physicality that held me so engaged, although undeniably enthralling.

No, it was the symphony of emotions that surged forth—the passion that bound their souls together. For without the long build-up, the tension, the smoldering ember of desire, this act of intimacy would have been empty. A love that begins immediately is much less meaningful than one that is unexpected.

It was my kinship with these characters, cultivated throughout twenty-three riveting chapters, that transported me to an existence parallel to my own. A life where I wasn't Amara.

A life where I also felt a love so great that it consumed every part of my being.

As I found myself lost within the chapter, my racing heart thumped wildly against my ribcage, and the harsh intrusion of reality jolted me from my dreamscape. Three thuds echoed through my body, severing the connection I had made with the book.

I threw it to the side of me and laid it face down to keep my page number but also to hide what I was reading. My door then creaked loudly as it slowly opened wider.

"Sorry to interrupt." Arryn smiled as he made his way to the side of my bed eyeing the book obviously thrown to my side.

"It's fine. I was just about to go to sleep." I lied.

More like just about to go to sleep in three more hours when I finish this book.

"Do you need something?" I asked, fidgeting with the covers in a failed attempt to hide the top of the book.

"What are you reading?" He reaches for the book and swipes it from the bed. I quickly grab for it, but he's quicker than I am. My cheeks turn crimson and I can feel a lump form in my throat. He smiles and brings the book up to his face. I nervously observe his gaze darting from left to right, devouring each line with intent. As he progresses through the page, his eyes widen with what seems to be amusement.

"Give it back," I demanded, my anger surged forth, destroying any remnants of politeness. With a swift motion, I reached out and reclaimed the book from his grasp. The smile on his face waned as he detected the unmistakable traces of humiliation etched across my face. His gaze then trailed down, fixated on the expanse of my bare thighs peeking out from beneath my white nightgown. A moment hung there, filled with tension that could be cut with a knife.

I then drew the blankets up to my chin in hopes of shielding my form.

An embarrassment of two types now coursed through me. One was from the book he caught me reading, and the second was because I had been so exposed. The latter felt worse due to what I was already feeling from the book.

Despite my efforts to conceal, an inferno raged beneath my skin. I was now aware of the scorching heat, of the undeniable blush, staining my cheeks, an unspoken testament to what I was feeling inside from the book but also from humiliation.

His eyes met mine, and in that fleeting instant, I swear his head tilted, a tremor passed through him as if reason had momentarily abandoned him and now returned.

"I'm sorry." He headed back towards the door. "Goodnight, Amara." He turned back once more and offered a sympathetic smile before closing the door behind him.

As I laid back down, I let out a groan of embarrassment and then closed the book, ending my literary endeavors for the night. It was time to surrender to my tired eyes.

12

"Please. What do I have to do?" I begged the mysterious voice. It had no gender or name. Its sound was of many and it had no physical form. I was surrounded by darkness. Not one person, plant, or animal. Only the voice and myself. Complete and utter darkness.

"How do I get out?" I cried.

The voice laughed and then it began:

"In shadows' gentle grasp, she found her place,
   A glowing tree with pink blossoms, her saving grace.
   It cradled her with arms of light so pure,
   Yet she knew, in its warmth, she couldn't endure.

For it shielded her from the looming night,

That creeping darkness, an endless fight.
With gratitude, she left the tree behind,
As she embraced the path, her destiny aligned.

A cloud of darkness, the sun it did shroud,
  No fear remained, her heart unbowed.
  She reached out willingly, no longer in fright,
  Into the abyss, she vanished from sight.

A distant voice called, "NO!" in despair,
  But she cared not, for she was beyond repair.
  Into the darkness, her soul took flight,
  Extinguished, she felt nothing, eternal night."

My eyes flew open and the sweat spilling off me soaked the sheets. I steadied my breathing and looked around to scan the room to make sure I was truly awake. The sun shone through my windows, and I immediately knew it was over.

I just had to make sure it wasn't there. The voice. *The darkness.*

As terrified as I was, it was a recurring nightmare that I had been having for about a year. I had gotten used to its unwelcome place in my dreams.

After a few minutes, I calmed down and then threw on a robe to go downstairs. I pulled open the wooden door to my bedroom and crossed my arms, yawning, as I headed for the stairs. Just as I reached the second step, I heard muffled voices coming from the kitchen. I tried to make out what they were saying, but I could only tell that it was Arryn and Caris having a conversation.

   Getting closer wasn't an option because they would surely hear me with their enhanced fate hearing if I took one more step. I closed my eyes, focusing on their voices, trying to hone in on the words being said. I slowed my inhales and cleared my mind. Something clicked in my eardrums and it was as if I had given my sense of sight away to enhance my hearing.

   I heard a muffled voice that must've been Caris. "You can get out of it. You just need to reason with him…"

   Then the deeper voice, Arryn, replied "I know. It is a long trip to the other side of Nymyria, and my magic can only fly me so far… And I want to make sure that we are ready for him." I heard a grumble and took it as my cue to enter.

   When I scurried into the kitchen they both straightened and widened their eyes as if they were recalling what words they had just said and what I possibly could've heard. Good thing for them, I was too curious to keep it to myself. "Fly where?" I nervously looked between the two of them.

   Caris glanced at Arryn and him right back at her. I stepped closer to gain their attention back to me. My eyes darted between them both, beckoning for an answer. Finally, Arryn stood straighter and locked his eyes to mine. "It's nothing. We are just going to see my brother… trading plans and such."

Something in me sensed that simple trading wasn't the extent of this meet-up, but I wasn't sure that I wanted to get into family politics.

"You have a brother?"

"Yes," he replied shortly as he tightened his jaw. I could sense tension there. I knew what it was like to have family that caused you more pain than happiness. I decided not to pry further and changed the subject. I couldn't force someone to relive their painful past, even a fate.

"So..." I cracked a faint smile. "Where are we going, Caris?" I angled my head to face her. Her expression morphed into what only could be described as utter excitement.

❁ ❁ ❁

I should've stayed back at the house.

I had to admit, the scenery *was* breathtaking. We had passed several lakes and streams with fish of every color. Green hills surrounded us, and most of them were filled with wildflowers.

Even though it was my first time to see those things, I was clearly out of shape. Caris was far ahead of me since I had to stop to catch my breath multiple times.

We trudged through the forest of tall trees that seemed to reach the sky and then arrived upon two trees a doorway distance from each other. They hugged each other's weeping branches and formed a curve-like arch as if they were covering an imaginary gate to the field behind them.

Caris stood next to the arch waiting for me to catch up. "We're here!" Caris squealed before shifting to a laugh. "I'm glad you didn't pass out on me before we could make it here."

"Not much exercising underground, I guess," I joked, but she clearly didn't find it funny as her laughter stopped and her lips pursed.

She shook her head and once again plastered a big smile on her face as she sauntered through the archway. "Come on, I want to show you this."

I looked forward into the distance and furrowed my brows. "You do know that I know what grass is, right?" I said sarcastically as I took in the field in front of me. That's all it was. A field. Granted, there was no grass underground, but grass of all things was the least impressive thing of nature.

She threw her hands on her hips and tipped her head upward at me. "Just come on," she snapped while somehow still sounding pleasant.

I hiked all the way here and will be sore tomorrow just to see some grass.

I made my way to the arch and stepped through expecting an anti-climactic full view of the field. I stared with my eyes relaxed and my arms crossed as I made my final step through, clearing both trees. I was unimpressed, and I made no moves to hide it.

Just then, the wind started to murmur and sing in my ears as tiny orange flowers began to spring out from the grass, growing taller and taller as they had just woken up from a centuries-long slumber. There were so many that the sea of green was now fully orange.

"What—how?" I questioned as I looked around, utterly confused, but also amazed at the same time.

"Come, get closer to them, and *listen.*" She emphasized the last word and reached her arm towards me as she neared the flowers in front of us.

"'Listen?' How do you listen to a flower?" I laughed at her nonsense but followed after her nonetheless. She knelt and put her ear to the flower closest to her, and I followed suit.

For a moment, it was so silent I could hear my heartbeat, and then the same singing I heard when I walked through the gate danced around my ears, teasing me.

Sound swirled into my ears and I heard a hum of a voice. It wasn't deep or high-pitched, and it wasn't too loud or quiet. It was like a vibration that I could somehow make words out of.

"Amara is so beautiful. Her hair is long and the most perfect shade of brown. Dark and rich in color, with elegant curls. But her eyes are even more gorgeous. So blue that the sky doesn't compare."

I blinked and felt my cheeks turn a rosy pink. I turned to Caris, and she was also blushing.

"At least you know you're not ugly." She smiled as if she too had heard what the flowers had told me. "These flowers are called the whisps. They whisper secrets to you, starting small and progressively getting more... crucial to your life. But they are always true. The whisps can not lie."

She finger brushed her hair behind her ear. "I usually stop after the fourth one because I don't want to know that level of truth sometimes." She angled her face toward the ground and chuckled.

I faced the flowers again and let out a large sigh in awe. I should have not doubted her when she said to listen. At this point, nothing should surprise me after I saw the soul reaper. I shuddered but pushed away the memory.

"I have never seen anything like this," I said, reaching out to touch one, but before I could, Caris swatted my hand away.

"Don't touch them. They don't like it," she said with a stern glare. "The reason you can't see them before you walk through is because they are very slow to trust. When you walk through that arch, they decide if they deem you trustworthy or not of their secrets. When they are touched, they immediately lay back down, and who knows for how long."

She lifted her hand back from mine again. "But you're lucky. They seem to like you. I had never seen them stand up so quick for someone."

"Sorry, I didn't know." I sat back on my heels.

"Well, now you do." Her teeth twinkled through her wide grin. "You can listen to another if you want."

I nodded and returned the smile she bore me as I leaned down to listen to a different flower. Again, the vibrational dance teased my ear as I heard.

"Roses are your favorite flower, but we will top that soon enough."

I laughed, harder than I had in a long time. *Arrogant flowers.* As much as I hated to admit it, they very well had become my favorite the second I heard their first whisper.

I leaned in again for a third time and waited for the whisper.

"You were never meant to be underground so long. There is much more to you, and for you, Amara. Out in the world, you will see. Everything happens because fate deems it so."

I pulled back quickly and felt my eyes burn a bit as I swallowed back the lump trying to escape from my throat. I leaned in again to a different flower, the fourth flower.

"You and I are intertwined. Follow what you feel inside and the truth will be revealed. All will be revealed if you —"

Before I could hear the rest, I felt Caris pull me back and pull me up from the ground.

"We have to go. Now," she said sternly as she grabbed my hand and pulled me back through the archway. I hadn't noticed because I had been intently listening to the whisps, but a large, dark storm cloud rolled overhead.

Darkness fell upon the field and the wind began to pick up. I noticed instead of taking the path to get back to the castle, she was going the opposite way.

"Where are we going?" I yelled to her.

"The cottage. It's upon a lake just a few miles ahead. It's closer than the castle, and with the storm rolling through we have to take shelter!" she shouted back nervously.

It seemed like there was more to it than she was letting on. How dangerous could a storm be?

Nevertheless, I nodded and picked up my pace, following closely behind her.

I turned back once to see the storm, as I had never seen one before, and I noticed that there was only one storm cloud. It was headed toward the castle like it was on a mission.

I was knocked out of my thoughts when I bumped into a hard stocky figure. I turned around to see a familiar face and Arryn's arms grasped around me to keep me from falling.

"Follow Caris and stay with her. Do not leave, do not come back to the castle until I tell you to," he ordered me. "Caris, you drop her off at the cottage and then return to the castle immediately."

She nodded with no objections.

I looked up and into his melted gold eyes. "What's going on?" I asked looking between the two, still aware of his muscular arms tightly gripped around me. Now it was obvious that Caris *did* know more than she let on.

He gazed at me and then opened his mouth ever so slightly as if he was about to tell me, and then a loud crack of thunder sounded in the distance. He removed his arms and guided me towards Caris.

"Take care of her," he said as he faced her.

The wind swirled around us as another crack of lightning struck down with thunder booming in its wake.

"Go. Now," he ordered as a small plant shot up from the ground and propelled him in the direction of the castle. His ivy vines quickly sprouted into wings as he flew toward the storm.

I desperately wanted to know what was going on, but I valued my life more, so I reached out my arm letting my hand fall into Caris'. Without a second thought, I trailed behind Caris and didn't look back.

13

We entered the quaint cottage deep in the woods and the fireplace immediately sparked up. Most likely due to some magic placed on it.

Caris had her arms crossed and her knee was bouncing up and down in a nervous tremor while she showed me around quickly. "Okay, I'm off." She headed for the door.

"Wait, what's going on?" I reached for her arm to pull her back towards me. She pleaded at me with only her eyes as she angled her chin up. "Please."

"Arryn will explain everything." She placed her hand on the wooden door handle and looked back at me. "Be safe Amara. Do not leave this cottage under any circumstances. One of us will come for you." She smiled with her eyes and then she was gone.

I grimaced as I locked the door and turned around, sliding down against the wooden door until I was sitting on the cold damp ground.

The cottage was small, and fully made out of wood. It was run down, but comfortable. Random trinkets and items were scattered around and several candles were burning on each ledge on the wall and the table in the middle of the kitchen.

There were only two rooms, the kitchen that doubled as a sitting area, and one bedroom with a single bed and a rug on the floor that looked as if it was woven from various plants and vines.

I sighed and then looked out the tiny window covered with green drapes. There wasn't even any rain. Unbelievable.

They were hiding something from me. Whatever that was, they were scared of it.

But of course, they were hiding things from me. We had only just met, and it would be strange for them to tell me everything.

I thought Arryn *wanted* me to know everything, but again, I didn't *know* Arryn at all. He *was* a fate after all, and fates will play tricks on humans to get what they want. I just didn't know what he *wanted* from me.

For hours, I traded between staring at the fireplace, reading any book that I could find, and peeling off the shards of wood sticking up from the withering table to keep myself occupied.

 I checked the window every so often, partly out of boredom and partly to see if either Arryn or Caris had come to save me from it. I finally decided that I was going to head to bed when I was startled by a knock at the door.

 I raced over and lifted the heavy wooden bar from the door. I was too excited to leave that it could have been a soul reaper standing there and I gladly would've left with it.

 I swung the door open to reveal Arryn. He had a long cut along his jawline and disheveled hair.

 He looked exhausted, and not just physically. I could see the mental turmoil swirling around in his eyes.

 As I glimpsed Arryn's wound and the dark expression on his usually bright face, an unfamiliar worry enveloped me.

 It wasn't a concern for my well-being, but an unease that prodded at the edges of my understanding, urging me to do something to help him.

 I reminded myself that he was a fate. It was in their sinister nature to lie, trick, and provoke…but even though that's what I knew they were, it wasn't anything like I had observed the past few days. He had been kind, and Caris too.

I decided if I didn't *care*, then it would make me just like them. I wasn't above caring for others, even if they were fate.

I reached out to touch his jaw and I swiped the remaining blood with my finger. "Are you okay? What happened?"

"I'm fine. Let's go inside," he said as he walked past me.

I followed closely behind him and he turned around suddenly to face me. It was so quick I did not have enough time to stop as I thrashed into him. I placed my hands on his chest for support.

"Sorry," I flashed a faint smile and met his eyes with mine. His face was stoic as he grabbed my arms and helped me steady myself.

It was weird to see him with such a glazed expression. It was as if his mind was somewhere else completely. His usual self was so full of light, and his aura so bright, but in that moment, it was dull. His appearance so *off*, made me feel the same way.

"I owe you an explanation," he said, backing away a bit. "The storm earlier… I'm sure by now you figured out that it wasn't an actual storm."

I nodded as I damped a cloth and began to rub it over his jaw to clean the cut.

"It was my brother, Keiran. He's—he—" he stuttered and then took a deep breath. "He is not good. He is ruthless and cunning. He is all of the things that I despise, and—"

"And what?" My voice shook as I pulled the cloth away, setting it into a bucket in the corner.

"And he wants something that I don't know if I can give him right now." He looked down.

Fear began to bubble in my stomach. "What does he want?"

"We made a deal. One that I don't know if I can follow through with. I need time to figure everything out."

He took my hands in his as his eyes of pure gold met mine.

"He is dangerous, Amara. You need to be careful and you should not go anywhere alone. And especially, do not go out at night. He thrives in the darkness and can come and go undetected."

I wanted to argue. To tell him that I could handle it and fend for myself, but it wasn't true.

"Okay," I breathed. "I promise I won't go anywhere alone." The thought of him being concerned about my well-being made me feel nervous, and I didn't like it. "How does he do that? What magic does he have?"

Arryn sighed. "My brother, he is… *different*."

"Different how?"

Arryn took a seat at the table and motioned for me to sit as well. "Our parents fell in love, even though they were from two different worlds—*kingdoms*. My father was from here, the Kingdom of Light, and my mother was from the Kingdom of Darkness.

"The fates who are born here inherit their powers from the sun, from light, while the dark fates draw power from the darkness."

He ran his fingers through his hair and then rested his chin onto his folded knuckles. "It is almost impossible for a dark fate to be born good. And the same with light fates; I have never seen an *evil* one. My parents fell in love, and even though they loved each other, my mother was still extremely wicked.

"Wicked enough to kill my father and then herself when he told her he had fallen out of love." He sucked in a breath through his teeth before continuing.

"When my brother was born, it was apparent that he had taken after my mother, and then I was the opposite. It had been unheard of for a light and dark fate to unite, so no one knew what the outcome would be. Some speculated that we would be mutts. A mix of both light and dark magic, but we are the inverted versions of each other. Just like our parents."

I wanted to interrupt to ask more questions, but I figured I should just let him talk. Especially since this seemed so hard for him to speak about.

"As kids, we were close. He did not even show signs of being a dark fate, besides his ink-black hair and eyes. He was a happy, normal, child. It wasn't until—" He stopped and rubbed his forehead as if what he was about to say affected him more than he wanted to let on.

"It wasn't until our parents died… then he let the darkness consume him. It was almost like a switch flipped. He was never the same. Never felt any emotions, did not *let* himself feel them, or loved. Even almost two hundred years later."

The blood coursing through my veins froze. "Did you say, two hundred years?"

"Yes. I am two hundred and nineteen years old. My brother is a year older, not that it makes a big difference." He let out a shy laugh.

"Right," I said as I backed away in reflex. I nervously stroked my hair and twisted it around my finger and said nothing for a few moments.

"I'm sorry about your parents—" Even though I was trembling and I could hardly process what I was hearing, I genuinely meant it. "And your brother."

He nodded in appreciation but kept his gaze pinned to the ground.

"Well," he said standing up and looking around the small cottage. "We better get to bed. It's late."

I stood up in response and made my way to the front door. I was eager to be going back to the castle.

"We are staying here for the night," Arryn clarified.

I whirled around and exposed a pleading wince. "Why can't we just head back now?"

He smiled at my request. "It's late and it's very dark. If my brother comes back, we won't be able to sense him until it's too late. It's also a few hours-long hike back. Plus, there are much worse things than soul reapers on these lands."

Shuddering at the thought of something worse than a soul reaper, I replied, "Like what?"

He was silent for a moment as if he debated his response, "There is another form of magic. One that doesn't come from light or darkness. Those who wield this unnatural form of magic are called fate weavers. That's what they like to be called, but you might know them better as witches."

Witches?

I remembered back to when Mason lied that I had bewitched him and how that would have been a crime underground. Here, even the witches were able to roam free.

Shifting my focus back to the problem at hand, I responded, "Can't you just use your plants to fly us back?" I probed. "Or use *magic* or something?"

He let out a low chuckle. "I can only fly so far. I could probably get us only a mile before my magic is depleted. Especially since I would have to carry you too. We would have to go the rest of the way on foot."

I huffed and then nodded, not because I was truly scared of his brother finding us, but because I did not want to hike right now.

I hesitantly walked toward the bedroom when I realized there was only room for one person. "I can sleep on the fl—"

"I'll sleep on the floor." He grabbed an extra pillow from the bed and a throw blanket. He dropped his pillow onto the rug and laid down, pulling the blanket over top of him.

"Thanks." I grinned as I climbed under the covers and blew out the candle sitting on the small table beside the bed.

Another memory from the underground flashed through my head.

Candles everywhere. The only type of light that existed was from flames. I pushed the thought away and rolled over on my side facing where Arryn was lying on the floor.

"Did he put that cut on your face?" I wanted to revive the conversation as I knew I wasn't going to be able to sleep just yet.

"Yes," he answered.

"How?" I pressed.

"You ask a lot of questions," he replied. His tone was light and airy. As if he wasn't meaning to be rude, but just stating a fact about me like he just learned it.

"There's a lot to ask," I said in a tone that would remind him that this wasn't my world.

"The thing he wants from me, I told him I didn't have it yet. Then, he threatened me and held a knife to my throat. Even though it was a scare tactic, when he actually pressed the blade into my skin—" He shuddered. "I saw it in his eyes, that he wouldn't hesitate to kill me to get what he wants."

I stayed silent for a moment not knowing what to say in response.

Do I offer sympathy? Do I try to say something that will help him cope with the fact his brother is heartless?

Do I ignore his agony since he is a fate?

"What does he want from you?" I blurted out, choosing to keep being inquisitive instead.

"I think it's time we go to bed." I heard his blanket rustle as he turned over.

I rolled my eyes even though it was too dark for him to see it.

🌹 🌹 🌹

I woke up from the reoccurring nightmare that plagued my dreams for more nights than I would like to admit.

It was still pitch black outside, from what I could tell looking out the small window in the bedroom. It must have been the middle of the night. I sat up as my eyes adjusted and I looked over to the ground beside my bed. I could make out the pillow, and Arryn's head wasn't lying on it.

I couldn't help my curiosity, so I tiptoed out of bed and twisted the doorknob gently so it didn't make a noise.

As I peered into the kitchen, I saw Arryn sitting at the table with a candle lit beside him.

There was a book open out in front of him and his head was leaned back against the wooden chair.

"Arryn?" I whispered.

No response.

I tiptoed over to the table and peeked around so that I could see his face. His eyes were shut and his mouth was ever so slightly parted.

I smiled and took the book he was reading into my hands.

No wonder he fell asleep.

I chuckled mentally as I read the title *"Soil and Seeds."* A book about gardening.

I stepped over to one of the plants sitting on the ledge and plucked a green leaf from it then walked back to the table and placed the leaf into his book on the page he left off on then closed it shut.

I looked at him once more before I crept back into the bedroom and grabbed his pillow from the floor.

He gave me a place to stay, the least I could do was give him a pillow.

Silently, I stepped back over to him gently lifted his head off the back of the chair, and slipped the pillow underneath.

His silver hair was draped over the front of his face, covering the left side of his forehead and eye.

I brought my hand up to reach his cheek as I brushed aside his glowing locks. I stared at him for a few minutes, my hand still fiddling with his hair.

I wasn't quite sure what I was doing, but it felt… *good*.

I didn't want it to, but looking at him… it was as if his light was radiating into me and filling an emptiness in my soul that I didn't even know that I had.

Every inch of me pulsed with a warmth that spread from my fingertips touching his skin. His light, the Light Kingdom… it was—

It was beautiful.

Full of wonders that I didn't even know existed. I hadn't even seen the half of it yet, but in the two days I had been there, it was the most alive I had ever felt.

I hated to admit it.

I hated that I was right. That all along, that incessant tug on my soul all those years, knew.

Knew that there was a whole world I had been missing out on.

Yes, it was dangerous and scary, but it was worth it.

Observing him in slumber, I started to discern that his looks were indistinguishable from mine, that of a human. He possessed lips, eyes, hair, and all the features of a human being. He experienced emotions, and required sustenance and rest, just like us. The sole difference lay in his possession of magic, but did that inherently imply that he was evil? I hadn't witnessed any actions that would say otherwise, and truth be told, I've genuinely enjoyed my time here.

I didn't want to love it here.

I wanted to hate this place and hate him, but everything about this land, about him and Caris, it was so bright. It something I had never fathomed underground.

Yes, he is a fate, but he was just like me.

A person who *feels* and wants to *live*.

How could I continue calling him and his kind evil when I hadn't actually observed anything evil at all?

Underground, we were taught to fear magic, but maybe the humans were scared of it because they just didn't understand it.

I don't even understand it, but I think now I might want to.

I scanned his face, the ridge of his nose, and how perfectly it came to a stop and tipped up into a rounded point.

His eyes were perfectly spaced from his nose. His lips were arched in a cupid's bow and the most delicate shade of pink. They looked soft and welcoming.

I couldn't help but wonder how they felt.

Did they feel like mine? Like a mortal's? Or were they different? Did they feel as supple as the petals on a rose?

I brought my hand from his hair to cup his cheek and then I grazed his lips once with my thumb.

Of course, they would be soft as a rose petal.

I smiled and then grabbed a book off the shelf as I headed back to bed before he woke up and wondered what I was doing.

The truth was, I had no idea either.

🌹 🌹 🌹

I opened the black-covered book with silver sparkling flecks all over it.

The title was *"Moonlit Myths: Tales From the Land of Midnight."*

I opened the first page to see it was decorated with wonderful illustrations around each page. I looked at the first line of the story and started to read.

The Tale of
LUMINARIA

Once upon a time, in a land shrouded in the legends of darkness and whispered tales of wickedness, there lay a village named Luminaria. It was nestled beneath the vast, ancient Shadowpeak Mountains, and its people were believed to wield a magic so dark that even the gods who made the world were scared of it.

Outside Luminaria, travelers spoke of the eerie enchantments that surrounded the village, tales of shadows that danced and ghostly apparitions that roamed the nearby forest. It was said that anyone who entered the village would either never come out, or they would never be the same. Fearful rumors persisted, painting the villagers as wicked sorcerers of the night.

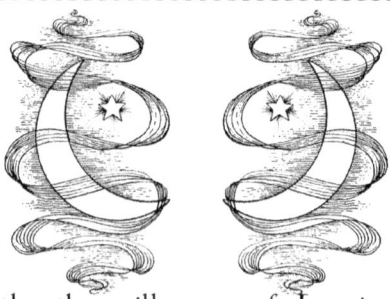

In truth, the villagers of Luminaria were gentle souls who cherished the silver glow of the moon. Each night, they gathered atop the tallest Shadowpeak mountain, where a great crystal, the Moonstone, stood tall and luminous. This radiant gem, a gift from the heavens, reflected the light from the moon and bathed the village in a soft, ethereal light.

The villagers of Luminaria had no magic of darkness. Instead, their enchantments were born from the gentle caress of moonlight. They could weave moonbeams into melodies that played like silver symphonies and create shimmering illusions that sparkled like stardust. Their magic was used to heal, to bring joy, and to nurture the land around them.

One fateful night, a wanderer named Elara stumbled upon Luminaria, guided by tales of its ominous reputation. She wanted to see for herself if the village was everything that people made it out to be.

As she entered the village, she expected to find witches casting spells and evil potions being brewed. To her surprise, she encountered warmth and kindness. The villagers welcomed her with open arms, inviting her to join them in their Moonlight Festival. They never had visitors before, and everyone was overjoyed that someone finally ventured into their village beyond the mountains.

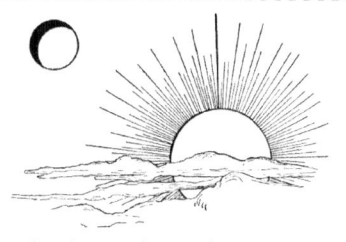

> Underneath the celestial canopy of the night sky, Elara watched in wonder as the villagers performed their enchanting moonlit dances.
>
> Elara chose to stay in Luminaria, and her presence helped dispel the misconceptions that had cast a shadow over the village. With time, the world learned that the people of Luminaria were not bearers of darkness but guardians of moonlight, and their hearts radiated with kindness.
>
> And so, the village of Luminaria continued to thrive, its enchantments gracing the world with a gentle, silvery magic that whispered the truth: that even in the darkest of places, the light of goodness and love could always shine through, if one dared to look beyond the shadows."

I had been half-asleep when I read the last paragraph and could hardly keep my eyes open to shut the book. Something about a good story before bed always made every single nerve in my body relax and turn warm.

Before I knew it, my whole world had turned to darkness as my eyes succumbed to the soothing embrace of slumber.

14

When I awoke, The Tale of Luminaria was still spinning through my thoughts as it was the last thing I had done before I fell asleep. Then, I remembered what brought me to read the book in the first place.

I remembered giving a pillow to Arryn and…

Oh god.

The pangs of anxiety rushed through me as I remembered how I had caressed his cheek and brushed his hair back from his forehead while he was asleep.

And touched. His. Lips.

I didn't feel embarrassed at the moment, but now… now that the moment was upon us, I was terrified to see if he had truly been asleep or not.

If he had woken up and saw me—

I didn't let myself finish that thought as I was too nervous to even think about the possibility.

I didn't know what I was thinking. For the first time, it had occurred to me that not everything I was taught about the world above was true. The shock of that realization caused me to act in that way… but I suspect the romance book from the other night also had something to do with it, causing me to have thoughts that hadn't entirely been of my fruition.

I only knew the genre of these types of books because I had told Caris about it on our hike to the Whisps. She laughed when I said I was lost for words and that I had never seen a book like it before. She then told me that they were called romance books and that she secretly had read that same one as well. I guess that explained why it was even on the bookshelf.

However, at my core, I knew that it wasn't really because of the books. I was a person filled with wonder. It is only natural for me to want to learn about this new world and the fates that I spent my entire life hating.

"Good morning." I blushed as I took a seat at the kitchen table. My nerves almost caused me to stay in bed until he gave up and left me there to rot. It would be better than facing him if he was awake last night.

"Morning. Did you sleep well?" he said with a kind smile, the same one he usually bore, and nothing about his expression was different from usual.

Good, he doesn't know.

"Yes, but I am guessing you didn't?" I gestured to the pillow sitting on the table and the blanket folded on the chair.

"No," he sighed as his eyes met mine. "You snore. Very loudly I might add." He let out a short laugh.

My eyes widened and my cheeks turned crimson. "Sorry, I didn't know that, I could've slept out here if it was bothering—"

"Relax." He laughed. "I was kidding. I always have trouble sleeping, so I read the most boring book I can find and it knocks me out. Works like a charm every time."

My body eased at his words and I also let out a faint laugh. "You could've brought it into the bedroom."

"The floor was less comfortable than the chair," he retorted.

"I meant the bed," I blurted. He froze and gaped at me. I was even shocked at my own words, I didn't know where they had come from.

"I mean, you know, you could've slept there and I could've slept on the floor. We could've traded," I corrected myself.

"Right." He smiled as he took a bite out of the apple he had been holding. "One thing I wasn't sure about though—" He leaned back in his chair and gestured to the pillow on the table. "—Is how *that* was under my head when I woke up… Any ideas?" He grinned as he crunched another bite of apple.

"Nope. None. Maybe little fairies snuck in and gave it to you because they saw the horrible angle your neck was in and didn't want your head to roll off."

What did I just say? Little fairies?

A faint glow in my chest slowly started to replace the anger that I initially felt for him.

I wanted to learn more about him, and staring into his eyes made it a little harder to speak. I was afraid of sounding dumb or saying the wrong thing. Even though I knew he wasn't going to make fun of me, I didn't want to sound like an ignorant human who didn't know anything.

His smile took up most of the space on his face as he replied. "Yes, it must have been the *little fairies*." He emphasized the last two words as if he were telling me he knew who really had been behind it. "Next time, I hope they leave sugar cherries in their wake."

"' Sugar cherries?'" I questioned.

"You don't know of the tale of the sugar cherry fairies?" he asked with raised eyebrows. Not in a mocking way, but as if he was genuinely surprised.

"There's no way that there is a such thing as *sugar cherry fairies*,'" I scoffed.

"Oh, there is. Well—I haven't seen one personally, but the myths and fairy tales about them are convincing."

"What is the story?" I shamed myself for how excited I was to hear the story. How obvious it was to him that I did not know the tales in these lands. How much of an outsider I was.

He didn't make me feel that way though. He just showed me a gentle smile and spoke softly. "I will tell you all about them when we are back at the castle."

"When do we leave?"

"Now." He stood up and buttoned up the gold buttons on his white shirt. My throat went dry as I caught a glance of his chiseled form. His skin was a golden color, but with pink undertones unlike the color of his eyes that were practically pieces of the sun themselves. Every muscle on his chest and stomach bulged out. His body was slender, but all that was on his body was muscle.

I coughed to break my stare and then turned around to head for the front door.

"Perfect. I'm ready to go back to the castle—"

"We aren't going back there just yet," he mocked.

"Where are we going then?" I faced him once more.

"I want to show you something first."

I followed Arryn as we strode into a town where I immediately smelled a sweetness wafting through the air. It was a scent so pure it was as if happiness had taken form of a sugary treat.

As we walked deeper into the town square, what I saw made my breath catch.

There were several shops selling everything from books and art to food stands that sold sweets and other goodies. The walkways were paved with iridescent stones that seemed to softly glow as if they were kissed by the sun itself. Above the shops, lanterns were strung from roof to roof. At night, I assumed that they would provide a warm light that made the town feel even more magical.

Suns were plastered everywhere. On every banner, lantern, and shop sign. The stones were even colored slightly differently to form one on the ground.

Although it was Autumn and the air should have been chilly, the town felt warm and inviting. It felt as if I was sitting in front of a fire. The warmth enveloped my body and hugged my skin.

"This is—" I couldn't finish my sentence as I looked from shop to shop, not knowing which I wanted to stop into first.

Arryn smiled and then inclined his head forward. "After you," He said.

"Really?" I questioned.

"Yes, really. Just go wherever you please, and I will be right behind you."

I grinned widely and bit my lip to hold back a squeal that almost escaped from me.

I had never seen a place like it. I mean, of course, I hadn't, but I never dreamed there could be such a magical town filled with such light. It was like something from a storybook.

It didn't feel real.

I was scared to close my eyes in the small chance that I *was* dreaming and would awaken back in my chambers underground.

Then I thought of Poppy. As much as I missed her and wished she could have been there with me, I wasn't sure she would enjoy it. Most people underground were content with their lives. They didn't yearn for more, they did not even care that there was a whole world out there. Most times, I wished that I was like them, that I did not wish for more.

But in that moment, I was happy that I did. Happy that my mind *was* that way. For the first time ever, I appreciated the insistent thoughts that reminded me that there had to be something better.

Then I thought of my mother. She hadn't even been there when I was banished. As much as I wanted to be upset at her for not standing up for me, how could she? How could she when it was all she knew? She didn't know what I dreamed of more than anything was a *life*. A real life where I could experience all there is to offer in this world. Part of me hoped I had gotten it from her, that I wasn't alone in my strange thinking, but even until the end, she showed no signs.

"I want to go there first." I pointed toward a bookshop named *"Enchanted Books and Scrolls."* As we entered, I realized the name of the shop had been quite fitting since there were quite literally enchanted books and scrolls gently floating and rotating in the air. Shelves weren't needed in this shop as the books held their places in the air all by themselves.

I passed by several books that told tales of romance, adventure, and fairy tales of princes and princesses. I turned around to ask Arryn if we could buy one but he was gone.

I roamed through the aisles until I spotted his shining silver hair. It was similar to others in the town, but he shined the brightest. Other fates in the town had bright hair, but most shades ranged from honey brown to golden blond. None were quite like his.

He stood with his back turned towards me as he examined a book.

"Did you find something?" I asked, and he jumped at my voice. He turned around in a swift motion and held something behind his back. I could have sworn I saw a pink flush over his cheeks too.

"No, nothing… do you want to go get something to eat? I will be right there, I just have to find something for Caris first." He pulled out some silvers from his pocket and handed them to me.

"Okay, sure." My heart sank a bit at the fact he wouldn't be joining me, but I was still ecstatic to try the treats of the different food vendors.

My nose led me to a small cart with a sign that read *"Sunlit Sweets."* I watched the cart owner as he pulled out two crystalline candies, that sparkled like diamonds and handed them to the customers in front of me.

"What can I get you, Miss?" the old man with white hair questioned from behind the cart.

"I will just take one of those," I said, pointing to the same candy the people in front of me purchased.

"Coming right up." He handed the candy to me as I handed him a silver.

"Thank you!" I flashed a wide grin as I strode away with my treat.

I felt like a kid in a candy shop for the first time. Well, an adult—who is forced to live in a land of magic and fates—in a candy shop.

As soon as I took a bite of the crystal candy, it melted on my tongue immediately. It turned to a liquid that emitted a burst of sweet sunshine flavor that coated my entire mouth. It was like nothing I tasted before. It was as if drops of sunshine had been mixed with sugar and formed into small diamond shapes.

I heard a laugh from behind me and I spun around to see Arryn standing there. His smile was so wide I wasn't sure it was me who he was smiling at.

"Are you enjoying that?" he laughed as he took a few steps toward me.

"Yes, very much," I admitted.

He laughed even harder when I spoke.

"What?" I chuckled.

"Your teeth." He laughed in between his words as if he couldn't contain himself.

I ran to the nearest vendor who sold hats and headbands made from wildflowers and looked into the hanging mirror. My teeth were—

They were glowing yellow, so bright it was like staring into the sun.

"You ate the sundrops, didn't you?"

"Um… I guess?" I replied as if I was asking a question.

"Those are my favorite. I don't even care how ridiculous they make my teeth look."

"Here, I have one left!" I said as I held out the piece of candy to him.

My whole body tensed as he leaned forward and brought his face to my hand as he took the candy out of my fingers with his mouth. His tongue accidentally brushed against my thumb as he pulled back. I was sure that my face was beet red now. A sickness swirled in my stomach that made me feel as if I fell twenty stories down from a tower.

His eyes met mine as he chewed the candy.

"What now?" he said smiling wide to reveal his glowing yellow teeth.

He was right, it did look ridiculous, but the taste was too good to pass up.

I opened my mouth and it was an effort to get any words out. "I saw an art shop earlier. I would like to go there before we leave."

"Let's go then," he responded as he gave me his arm to hold. I reluctantly wrapped my arm around his, my skin rubbing against the cool fabric of his sleeves. His arm was like stone beneath mine. I imagined how impossible he would be to beat in a game of arm wrestling.

When we entered *"Aurora Art,"* I was proven wrong once again. I thought I had seen everything, but to my surprise, it was a magical art gallery. There was a wall of blank canvases where if you walked by one, the canvas would paint either your fate or your deepest desire. I watched as a woman with her small child walked by one and they were turned into a painting of a queen and a princess staring out from a tall tower.

"Try it," Arryn said, nudging me forward.

"I don't know if I want to see what it would paint for me." I joked even though it was partially the truth. I wasn't quite sure that I wanted to know my fate or even what my deepest desire was. I had no idea of either and I was content with it staying that way.

Curiosity is one thing, but I didn't want to spoil my life for myself.

"Well, if you won't then I will." He moved past me to the tallest blank canvas.

He stood relaxed as the painting began its magic. Colors of silver, gold, yellow, and white began to appear on different spots on the canvas, and in just a few short moments it had become a painting of Arryn. It looked as if he was staring into a woman's eyes and holding her hands. His eyes were full of love and promise. A promise to never stop loving her.

The painting continued and more colors began to fill in the outlined woman. Every minute a new feature was discernible. She had dark brown, almost black, hair with loose curls, faint freckles scattered across her nose and tops of her cheeks, blue eyes—

My heart leaped and danced as I peered into those eyes.

My eyes.

Arryn and I must have had the same revelation at the same time as he practically ran away from the canvas. The paint disappeared from it and once again it was blank.

"We should go." He reached behind his head and scratched his neck in an awkward attempt to change the conversation and a bashful shade of pink stained his cheeks.

"Yes, we should." My words were breathy as it was hard to inhale.

Does that mean that he…No, it can't be. It wouldn't make any sense-

"I will go get the carriage," he said, hastily making his way out of the shop. Thankfully we had taken a carriage into the town so it gave him an excuse for us to not talk about what we just saw.

I contemplated following after him in case it only took a few minutes to get the carriage ready, but a magnetic pull of some sort was begging me to look in the back of the shop. It went on for aisles, and I was curious as to what else was back there.

I ventured down the aisles, and fewer customers were in each one the further I went back.

It felt like the shop was endless in length before I finally reached the last aisle.

It was pitch black.

There was less light further back into the shop, so the last aisle was too dark to even see the paintings.

I walked down it anyway and all the way down, I saw a pair of silver glowing eyes staring back at me.

I stumbled backward as those silver eyes became bigger as if whatever, whoever it was, was taking steps towards me. I fell into a few canvases on the shelf next to me before I backed up into the wall. The middle aisle was the way to get out and head back to the front of the store, but he was now in front of it, blocking my only exit.

I was trapped. Backed into a corner.

No. I wouldn't be trapped. Not again.

I grabbed one of the paintings nearest to me and swung it out in front of my body as if it were a sword.

"Come any closer and—"

"And what?" a male's voice purred. It sounded like liquid velvet.

"I will use this. I will hit you with it!" I said, swinging the canvas back and forth once to show I wasn't bluffing.

Before I knew it, his cold hand was clenched around my wrist and the canvas was now in his other. He pressed into me, my back crushed against the wall. His silver eyes glowed in the darkness and as his face was now mere inches from mine, I could only make out some of his features as there was hardly any light.

His hair was tousled and jet black, but seemed to gleam with an ebony sheen. It was parted in the middle and fell in sleek waves.

His jawline was sharp and his cheekbones were perfectly sculpted. Lips so full and far too close to mine for my liking.

Every move he made exuded confidence and his build was strong and slender, similar to that of Arryn's.

He wore all black clothing and the power that radiated off of him made every bone in my body tremble. It was almost like I could feel the tendrils of his magic caressing my skin and studying my form.

"What do you want?" I steadied my breath to show him that I wasn't scared. Even though I was, he didn't need to have the satisfaction from knowing it.

"Hm, funny you should ask that." Before I knew it, his teeth connected with my arm and pierced through my skin. Not deep enough to cause immense pain, but deep enough that I let out a small yelp. I winced and pulled back my bloodied arm. Two small holes now lay in the middle of the underside of my forearm, blood dripping out and down my wrist.

"Show him *this* and tell him that if he does not fulfill his end of our little bargain, I will *take* what's mine next time… No matter what war it starts." He released my arm and stepped back, his eyes morphing into a deep shade of black.

My eyes began to well up from the pain in both of my arms. One of them was bloodied, and one was bruised from his extremely tight grip. His eyes drifted towards where he held my arm, and then he pushed it away, finally releasing his grasp.

Just then we both turned our heads to the right, sensing a presence upon us.

A man—*a fate* stood there. His eyes were wide and his body frozen still as he gazed at the man next to me. He looked too overcome with fear to run away.

Before I could say or do anything, the man of darkness appeared in front of the stranger as if his body was made from darkness itself. He reached out his arms quicker than I could think and cracked the fate's neck sideways.

The sound reverberated through my head and sent a chill down my spine.

Bile rose in my throat and a scream stifled itself in the back of my throat as I was too stunned to speak.

My eyes burned with tears and now I didn't care about how quick my breaths were as my heart galloped in fear.

"You… you killed him. You killed that man—"

He turned to face me and then once again his body morphed to stand in front of me with a wide grin on his face.

"Yes, I did," he responded in a tone so calm it plucked at each of my nerves urging me to run.

But I didn't.

Forcing myself to ignore the dead fate to my right, I needed to know what was going on.

"How do you know Arryn? Who are you?" My voice was hoarse as I struggled to get any words out.

He let out a chuckle as his mouth curled upward into a feline grin. "Ask him."

Faster than I could reply, his body transformed into a cloud of shadow and dissipated into the darkness, leaving me with my blood-dripping arm, wondering what the hell just happened as tears rolled down my cheeks.

15

I practically sprinted out of the shop and back to the entrance into the town where Arryn was waiting with the carriage.

His smile dropped as soon as he saw the drips of blood falling from the bite on my arm and the wetness falling from my eyes.

It was like a river that I couldn't stop.

"What happened?" He raced towards me and immediately started unbuttoning his shirt and then when it was taking too long, he ripped the last half of buttons open and they popped from their seams.

He took my arm into his calloused hands and wrapped his shirt around the wound.

"I'm fine." His exposed top half almost made me forget any pain that I had been feeling, and any fear that remained from the encounter in the art shop. I could hardly remember what even happened as my gaze slid from his exposed chest to his torso.

His eyes followed where mine lingered and then his skin began to glow and shine, more than it usually did. There was a bright aura around his perimeter that seemed to be made from the sun itself.

My arm. Shit, my arm.

I snapped out of the paralysis that he seemed to put me in and winced as he pressed his hand harder against the bite.

"We have to get it to stop bleeding. I am sorry if this hurts, I am not trying to-"

"It's okay. I know," I replied with a slight smile.

"What happened, Amara?" he said in a soft tone that could only be described as concerned.

What happened? What happened…

No. That fate—

"We have to help him!" I whined as I felt my eyes widen when I remembered. "There was a man in the back of the art shop. I went to look at the last shelf because I was curious as to what was back there and… and there was a man. Waiting. He cracked that man's neck. He had these glowing eyes and—" I stopped as Arryn's face turned from gentle and worried to furious.

"What? What is it?" I asked.

"His eyes. Were they glowing silver?" His stare bounced between my eyes as if he was hoping I would say no.

"Yes."

He took a deep breath and then scanned the town around us. "We need to go. Now. You can tell me the rest on the way back to the castle." He flashed a small grin that I knew was only for my sake. I could tell he was only trying to lighten the mood so I wouldn't be frightened.

It didn't work, but the fact he cared for me in that way made me way too aware of the thumping beneath my chest.

"But Arryn, he hurt that man. We have to go see if we can help—" I pleaded.

"Amara… that man is *dead*. We have to get out of here. Now. Or we will be too." His face was a shield of determination as he gripped the sides of my arms.

I swallowed as I accepted his response.

I did see the fate die. His neck cracked and he fell to the floor… but part of me hoped there was still something we could do to help.

"Who was that?" I said afraid of what the answer might be. I hoped that I was wrong, but the way Arryn slumped and looked out the window towards the North, the Kingdom of Darkness, was answer enough.

He sighed and then began unwrapping the shirt from my wound so that he could put a clean spot over it. His fingers lingered on my arm longer than they should have, but not long enough for it to be spoken of.

When the shirt was fully off, I looked down at the bite that had now turned the area purple. Stemming down from the two bite marks were my veins. They had turned a purplish black color and were running down from the bites to look as if they were lightning bolts.

"Arryn, who did this to me?" I asked again as we both stared at the strange mark on my arm. Even though I already knew the answer, I needed to hear him say it.

His words sent a cold shiver down my spine.

"My brother."

🌹 🌹 🌹

Fury swirled in Arryn's golden eyes as I explained to him exactly what happened with his brother.

When I went over the part of his eyes glowing silver again, he became especially agitated.

"Why did he attack me, Arryn?" I stared out the window of the carriage taking in the scenery hoping that everything after the art shop had just been a bad dream.

"Amara, I am so sorry," he said without hesitating and clenched his jaw before sucking in a sharp breath.

Knots began to form in my stomach as his tone turned apologetic. "For what, Arryn?"

"My brother, Keiran."

Keiran. The name echoed in my head like thunder after a lightning strike.

"He made a deal with me…"

Keiran's words replayed in my mind as Arryn began to explain.

"Tell Arryn, that if he does not fulfill his end of our little bargain, I will take what's mine next time."

"He told me that he would leave the Light Kingdom alone. Forever… if I brought you to him. He would stop trying to take us over."

"What are you talking about?" I scooted away from Arryn as confusion swept over my face and betrayal settled in my stomach.

Me? What could he possibly want with me?

"I don't know how, but he somehow knew about you, knew what you looked like, what your name was, and that you were underground. He did not tell me how. He did not even say *why* he needs you, but I made the deal. I was desperate. I was sent to break you out and bring you to him." His voice wavered as he spoke.

"But as soon as I saw you banished, I immediately regretted it. I felt horrible and I couldn't believe he tricked me into doing something like that, I—I vowed that I would never bring you to him. That I would take care of you and protect you for the rest of your life. I even enacted a law and infused it with magic so that if you are brought outside of the Light Kingdom without your consent, it means war against the Dark Kingdom."

"Anger and betrayal were all I felt. I wasn't even scared anymore, only hurt that Arryn would do something like this. Our amazing day turned from incredibly sweet to painfully sour.

"Enacted a law? How are you able to do that?" I pushed past the anger to ask more questions. He was going to tell me *everything* now.

He sighed and closed his eyes for a moment. "I am the king of the Light Kingdom."

It was an effort to keep my mouth from dropping open. "King? And you didn't think to tell me? Or tell me *any* of this?" I was fuming by that point and it took everything in me not to rip open the carriage door and jump out just to get away from him. "*You. Sold. ME.*" I growled. "You are the reason I am here. In this mess. You take me to the town, and show me all these magical wondrous things… And it was all a lie. A solution to absolve your guilt."

Something like hurt flashed in his eyes. "I'm sorry," was all he could say. I suppose it was all I wanted to hear too because if he said anything else, I was going to scream. "But today was real. I wanted to spend time—"

"And I suppose your brother is the king of the Dark Kingdom then?" I snapped.

He nodded silently.

"Of course he is."

16

As much fun as our day was, I couldn't even be happy about it anymore.

How much of it was even real?

The entire day I thought that…

I don't know what I thought.

Maybe it was foolish of me to trust a fate. It was my fault to think that he could be good.

My flats pounded against the ground as I stomped into the house not even bothering to speak one word to Arryn on the way inside.

I glanced at his face before running inside and part of me broke at his bloodshot eyes and sullen dullness that took over his whole demeanor. His remorse was clear, but I still couldn't bring myself to accept his apology.

His sadness could just be another trick anyway. Any trust that he had earned was now completely gone.

"Caris. Take me somewhere, anywhere. Now," I begged her.

"Amara! You guys are back." Her rosy cheeks were plump from the smile she bore.

Her brows furrowed and her grin fell quickly when she recognized the anger that took over my face. "What happened?" she asked reluctantly. "I thought you two were going to have a nice day in the town?"

"We did. It was *nice*, and now it's not. I need to get out of here. Take me somewhere away from *him*, please," I said to her, not caring whether Arryn heard my harsh words or not.

It wasn't until that moment that I realized, *until I was out from the underground*, that when I was mad, I didn't care how sharp my words were. If I was wronged, then they most likely deserved whatever was coming to them. Harsh or not. I knew I would probably regret it later when I cooled down, but in the moment I had to say what was on my mind, and how I was feeling.

Caris looked at Arryn with a glare that screamed, *"What did you do?"*

And then she turned back to me. "Um, yeah sure. We can go on a walk—"

I cut her off. "No, too short. Too close to here. I want to be gone."

I felt bad for being so short with her, but I knew if I didn't get out right then… I wasn't sure what I would do.

I knew whatever friendship was forming between us was now ruined. Tarnished. I truly thought that he liked me, but I was just a pawn.

"How about the cottage?"

"Perfect," I said as I brushed past Arryn as I headed out the door, and my back brushed against his chest as I made my way out. His fingers gently caressed my elbow as if to say, *"I'm sorry."*

I ignored the warmth his touch provided me with as I continued marching away from the house, Caris on my heels.

I didn't bother to look back at Arryn. I already knew he was watching every step that took me further from him.

❦ ❦ ❦

We sat inside the small cottage drinking tea and talking about anything but Arryn. I didn't think I would be back here so soon. It was just a mere four hours ago that Arryn and I had left and I was already back.

It was midday when Caris and I arrived. We stopped to pick berries for a snack and then made oats with fresh honey.

"What happened?" I was waiting for her to finally ask me what was wrong. She had given me a lot of time to compose myself before inquiring about the situation.

"Well, Arryn told me about his little deal with his brother." I sipped my tea and searched her face for guilt.

Surely enough, it was there.

"I'm so sorry, Amara. I know I should have told you, but Arryn wanted to. I didn't want to mess anything up and—"

"It's okay. I'm not mad at you." Her face lightened a bit at my words. "I wish that you would have told me, but you're friends with Arryn first. I understand."

"Friends?" Her head perked up and all of the light returned to her eyes.

"That's what we are, aren't we?" My mouth slowly curled into a coy smirk and I shook my head as she giggled and reached her hand out towards mine.

Even though Arryn had been untrustworthy, I decided not to extend my feelings to Caris since she still had only treated me with kindness.

"I promise, I will treat you just as I treat Arryn from here on out. I want to be real friends. I will not favor him over you."

"Thank you, but I don't expect that from you. You have known him way longer and it wouldn't be right, but I will take you up on the part about being real friends."

She let out a sigh of relief. "So you know that he is the king then?"

"Yes." My tone shifted to something more sharp and hollow.

"He just wanted to protect his people from Keiran. I know that isn't an excuse, but… just try to see where he is coming from. That's all I am going to say about it. As for his brother… I almost hope that he tries something again so that Arryn can start a war against his kingdom and get rid of him once and for all."

The way she was speaking was so out of character for her. That's how I knew Keiran must have been as bad as they say. To make Caris so cold and unforgiving, I knew it would take a lot.

"What happened between them? Arryn talked a little bit about it. About his parents and everything, but he said Keiran used to be… *normal.*"

"There's a lot, and it's not my story to tell, but let's just say when their parents died, Keiran just… lost it. He snapped and gave into that darkness, and it swallowed him whole. He's numb and a shell of a fate. Arryn's heart breaks every day for what happened to his brother. Some days, I catch him gazing out towards the North with tears in his eyes. I never say anything though. Nothing I say could ever fix what he is feeling inside." Her voice turned grim as she finished.

Guilt immediately swarmed over my body, drowning the feelings of betrayal.

What Arryn did to me was wrong, but I felt so horrible for making everything about me.

I didn't stop for one second to think about how Arryn was feeling. How horrible it must feel to have a brother who tricks you into bargains only to keep your kingdom and your people safe. Keiran was pure evil, and Arryn was all that was good in the world. Yes, he was wrong for lying to me, but at the end of the day, he was only trying to do the right thing for his people.

We finished our tea in silence and then I stood up.

"Take me home, Caris."

🌹🌹🌹

I went straight to my bedroom when we got back to the castle. I was still upset at Arryn for lying to me, but I knew his heart was in the right place. He didn't know me when he made the deal, and it was for the good of his kingdom.

I wasn't even mad that he was king and didn't tell me.

Truthfully, I am not sure how I didn't figure out that he was king. The house, which was really a castle, should have been my first hint.

I didn't see Arryn as I walked through the castle, and I was glad. Even though I wanted to come back home, I still didn't want to see him. I needed time.

Caris and I had spent the whole day in the cottage and it was nightfall by the time we got back. Thankfully, we had just gotten home before the sun fully set.

When I shut the door to my bedroom and turned to get into bed, I saw a brown package with a golden string tied around it, forming a small bow on top.

Curiosity got the better of me, and I unwrapped it before I could even think of *who* had put it there.

As much as I tried to fight against my feelings, I couldn't help the smile and small giggle that escaped from me when I held the book in my hands.

It was a small storybook. *"The Tale of the Sugar Cherry Fairies."*

How did he get this?

We had just had the conversation that morning about the fairytale I had never heard of. He must have bought it when we were in the town.

Sneaky.

I quit trying to hold back the giddiness that swallowed me whole. He hadn't bought this to make me forgive him, he bought it before then. Before *everything*.

Completely ignoring the reasons why I was angry at him in the first place, I examined the beautiful cover of the book. The illustrations of fairies and the designs that swirled around the cover, gilded in a gold sheen, were breathtaking.

I hopped into bed, stretching my legs out as I held the book up above my face. I then opened the storybook to the first page and the interior was just as beautiful as the cover.

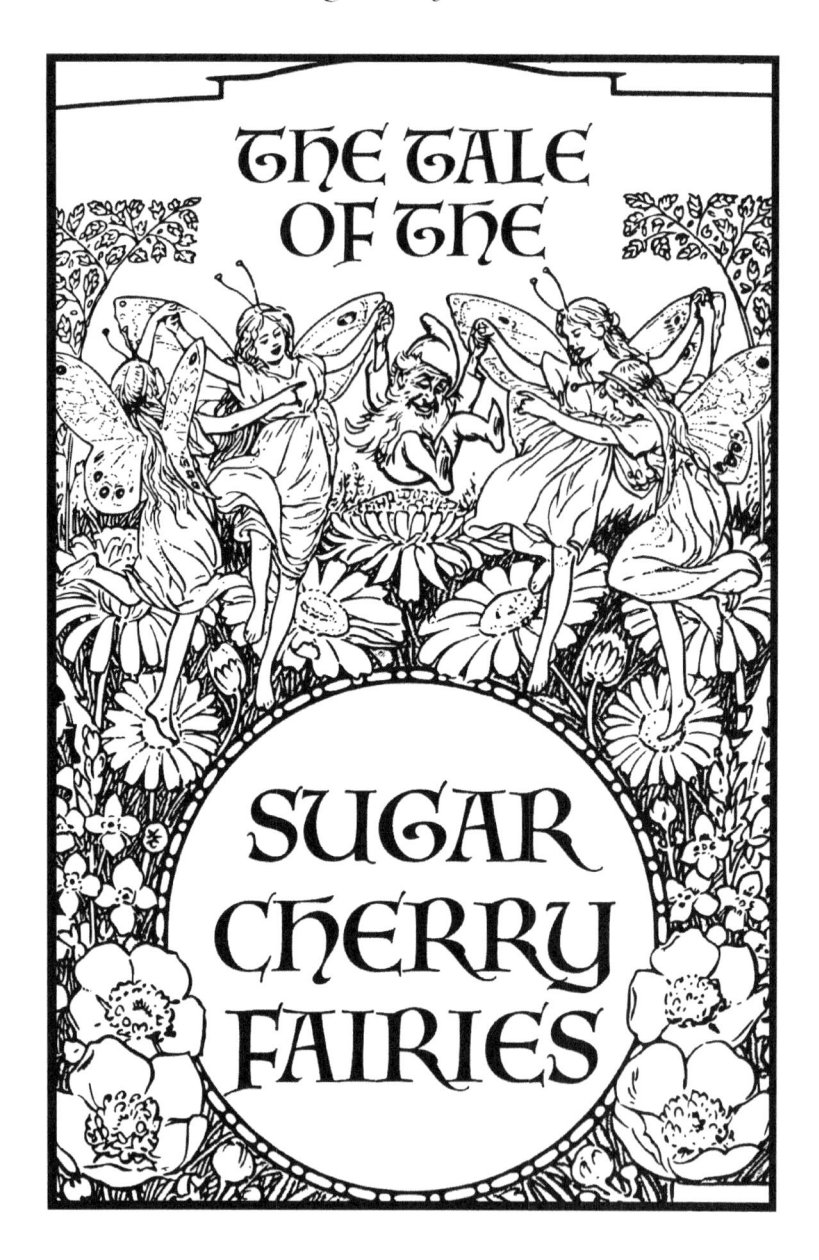

THE TALE OF THE SUGAR CHERRY FAIRIES

Once upon a time, in a hidden glen within the heart of the Enchanted Forest, there lived a peculiar clan of fairies known as the "Sugar Cherry Fairies." They were unlike any other fairies, for their wings sparkled like spun sugar, and their laughter sounded like the tinkling of a thousand wind chimes.

Among these fairies, there were two in particular: Rosalind and Jasper. They were inseparable, their hearts entwined like vines around a cherished tree. From the moment they met under the boughs of the ancient Sugar Cherry Tree, their love blossomed like the sweetest of nectars.

Every year, the Sugar Cherry Tree bore the most enchanting fruit known to fairykind. These radiant cherries were said to hold the power to reveal one's deepest desires. The fairies of the glen believed that eating a Sugar Cherry could reveal one's true love, but they had to be careful, for the cherries were rare and could only be picked on the night of the Sugar Moon.

As the night of the Sugar Moon approached, Rosalind and Jasper's excitement grew. They decided to pick a Sugar Cherry together, hoping it would affirm their love for each other. The moon rose high, casting a silver glow upon the glen, and the Sugar Cherry Fairies gathered beneath the tree.

Rosalind and Jasper each plucked a ripe cherry from the tree's branches, and as they took a bite, their hearts swelled with anticipation. To their amazement, the cherries revealed not only their love for each other but also a shared dream ~ to spread the magic of their Sugar Cherry Tree.

Wanting to share this gift of the sugar cherries with the world, they decided that every year they would leave their magical cherries on the doorstep of those who needed its magic most. Or, they could be summoned by a heart drawn on the front door with the initials of the lovers who wish for the cherries magic.

The sugar cherries helped lovers find one another, mended broken hearts, revealed deepest desires, and filled the air with an enchanting sweetness that brought joy to all who inhaled it. Its taste, was said to be so sweet that the person who ate them would never be able to eat any other dessert or fruit again.

As for Rosalind and Jasper, their love only deepened with each passing day. Under the boughs of the Sugar Cherry Tree, they celebrated their love, their dream fulfilled, and they lived happily ever after, surrounded by the sweet magic they share with the world.

And so, the legend of the Sugar Cherry Fairies became a symbol of love and magic, reminding all who heard the tale that love could be as sweet and enduring as the most precious of cherries.

THE END

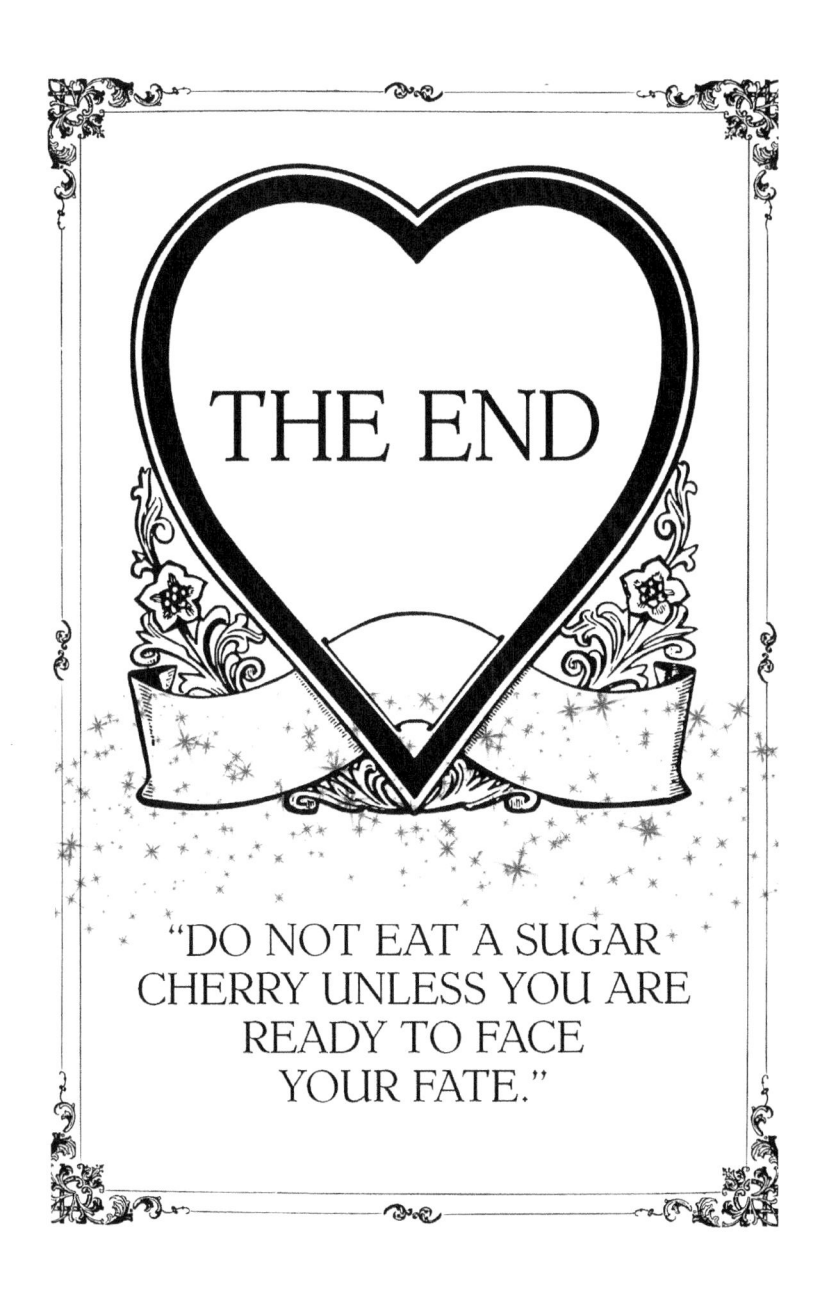

"DO NOT EAT A SUGAR CHERRY UNLESS YOU ARE READY TO FACE YOUR FATE."

17

I wandered through the castle checking room after room for Arryn. I ran into a few maids on the way there and they all looked at me as if I had three heads.

The way I was marching through the hallways, I probably did look a tad unhinged.

I reached the end of the hall where ivory double doors stood with vines curling around them and golden door knobs.

Taking the chance it was Arryn's room, I barged in and beheld the white furniture and walls with gold accents. There were gold swirls on the wall and embellishments on every item in the bedroom. It was twice the size of my own and it had a living area that led to the actual bedroom.

I walked through and it was then that I spied Arryn standing on his balcony, looking out at the night sky.

He sensed me before I could say anything and he turned around, eyes shimmering with hope and remorse.

"Amara—"

"Let me talk," I said in a smooth tone as I raised my hand to stop him. "Even though what you did was wrong, I can't expect anything from you." His brows raised as I continued. "We didn't know each other when you agreed to his deal. Plus, I can't really blame you for agreeing when it would protect your kingdom. I might have even done the same thing if it was up to me…"

"But from here on out, please do not lie to me again. Do not tell me half-truths or omit information that you know would upset me. Of course, I shouldn't have expected this from you before, but now—" I paused before I said something I hadn't yet faced myself.

"Now what?" he questioned as he stepped closer to me, closing the gap between us.

"Things are different. I consider you a friend."

"Friends with a fate?" he smiled and rested his arms behind him on the rail.

"Don't make me regret it." I returned his smile before continuing in a stern tone. "Seriously though, no more lies. No more secrets."

An expression crossed over Arryn's face, one I couldn't quite recognize, but it was gone as soon as it appeared. "No more secrets," he replied.

"Good… and since we are here, I wanted to thank you for the book. Now I can spend the rest of my life wishing for a sugar cherry to tell me who my true love is." I laughed.

"You know… the sugar cherries aren't fully a fairytale. Well, they are, but there is something quite similar in the fate lands… " He paused.

I stayed silent waiting for him to continue.

"Well, are you going to tell me what it is?" I finally begged. I crossed my arms and tilted my head in annoyance as I waited for him to finish.

His mouth curled upward into the widest grin. "There she is."

"What?" I furrowed my brows.

He chuckled and then shook his head as he lifted his hand to his mouth and brushed his lip with his thumb and forefinger.

He ignored my question and then continued. "It's called the Orb of Fate. When a fate turns twenty, they are given the option to see into this orb, only once. That is the only time we are ever allowed to peer into it, to see a glimpse of our fated match, something about them or something that they like. Think of it as a hint, a little bit of information about your match that you can use to find them. A clue in a lifelong treasure hunt. It is offered once on our twentieth birthday, and never again. We can either accept the orb or turn it down, letting fate surprise us."

"Fated match?" I scrunched my brows together in question.

"Yes, every fate has one. Sometimes we never meet them, sometimes we do. A soul that has been matched to ours so perfectly by the universe…" His eyes wandered my face and neck as he stepped closer to me.

"Some say, fated matches are one soul split into two. In this world, when they find each other again, it is like finding the other half of yourself," he said with longing eyes as if he yearned for his other half.

I couldn't help but remember the matching ceremony underground and how different it was from this beautiful process. How opposite these two ceremonies were from each other. One built on greed and necessity and the other on love.

One was a required union. Two people joining together for prosperity. Not because they can't imagine a world without the other or because they feel as if they are the other half of their soul… *no*. It was a cruel process. A process that I knew was wrong. It always felt wrong…

Being in Nymyria, I realized that love can not flourish without choice. True love can not be forced or created. It is something that is out of our control.

Who we love is chosen before we are even born, and the fated match process proves that who we are meant to be with is entirely up to fate.

"Did you do it- Look into the orb?" I asked him.

"No," he answered immediately. "I didn't want to know. I wanted things to happen naturally without me searching for the one hint all my life. Some fates spend eternity searching for their match with the hint given to them. It drives some mad, and I didn't want that fate for myself."

I stirred over his words for a few moments before asking another question. "How do you know when you have met your match? Is it some magical feeling that makes you blind to all others?"

"Something like that." His golden eyes gleamed as they met mine. "I haven't experienced it yet, but I have heard it is either right away or sometimes when the two… unite for the first time." He gently slid his tongue over his bottom lip. "Sometimes it takes time for it to click into place and sometimes it's immediate. It is different for every fate and how open they are to it."

A strange sensation bloomed in my chest at the fact he hadn't found his yet. Relief caused me to let out a sigh and relax my tense shoulders.

"Well, again, thank you for the book. It was… sweet of you to buy it for me," I said as I reached out my hand to caress his arm in appreciation.

"You're welcome." He looked down and when he viewed the dark veins still marked on my arm his face fell into a frown.

I looked down my arm and then covered the marking with my other hand. "Why did he do that, anyway? Bite me, I mean."

Arryn tensed before crossing his arms. "He just wanted to piss me off."

I widened my eyes to urge him to continue speaking.

He sighed and then said, "It is just a very… *intimate* thing that fates do."

"Intimate? How? You mean he enjoyed my blood or something?" I joked and let out a small laugh. When I looked back at Arryn's face and saw he wasn't laughing I realized I may have been a little too accurate.

"Oh…"

Oh.

It was then that I remembered the small canines that poked out from Arryn's mouth anytime he smiled wide. They weren't long, but they were sharp.

"So fates… drink blood?" I gulped so loud it was almost embarrassing.

"Not really. It is more of a delicacy that enhances whatever we are feeling in that moment. It isn't needed for us to live, but we do enjoy it on… certain occasions. Like I said before… it's an intimate thing."

"Right." I nodded as I rubbed the bite mark from Keiran, wishing I could heal the wounds faster.

He reached forward and took my hands in his as his thumb caressed the side of my palm. "I am sorry for getting you into this mess. I will never forgive myself, but I promise to protect you. I won't let anything happen to you ever again."

My stomach danced with a delicate flutter like a kaleidoscope of butterflies suddenly awakened by his words.

Even if his need to protect me was carried on by some guilt from him causing this in the first place, I couldn't help but feel like there could be more to it than that.

18

It had been a few weeks since Keiran left that mark on my arm. The black veins lightened in color, but they were still there. It was like he had put a little piece of his darkness into my blood.

Arryn had said later that when fates… *do that*, they wear the marks proudly on themselves so everyone knows who they are with.

The fact Keiran felt as if he could claim me in that way just for fun to piss off Arryn made my blood boil.

Arryn also put several plans in place the past few weeks for if, *when*, Keiran returned to take me.

And he would. It was just a matter of time.

I didn't understand why he didn't just take me the other day, but then Arryn explained that in addition to the law that he enacted, he also put magic over me so that if Keiran tried to take me anywhere against my will, he would turn to stone. Thanks to Caris' special magic of petrification, she and Arryn were able to fuse their magic together to put an enchantment on me.

The enchantment protected me against Keiran, but it only lasted so long. Enchantments only work for as long as the magic lasts, Arryn said. When it runs out, the magic will be gone. Especially with how powerful Keiran was, he would be able to break the enchantment quickly with his magic. We had to figure out another way to stop him for when it would inevitably give out.

I hadn't seen Arryn in a few days because he had some king business to attend to. I wouldn't admit it to him or anyone else, but I seemed to miss his presence. Dinners and lounging around the castle without him there just wasn't the same.

I had stopped doing my hair and wearing nice clothes entirely. I usually braided my hair or put it into a neat updo in addition to wearing frilly dresses. Without him walking around it just seemed pointless.

Not that I was trying to impress him, but I was not going to get all fancy just to lounge in bed and read all day.

I wore a silk golden colored nightgown that reached my mid-thigh and my long hair laid over my shoulders in a messy style.

Moments like that made teachings of the underground come back in a blur.

"There is always room for improvement."

It was hard for me to be so unpolished when we were taught that it was unbecoming to do so. It was hard to get out of the mentality of only making choices that would please a man. However, it was easy with Arryn because he never asked such things of me. He wasn't like the men underground.

He wasn't a man at all. He was a fate… but maybe the whole time I had it backwards? Maybe the humans were the ones to be feared.

Thinking of the humans made me think of Poppy for a moment. I missed her, but I knew she would be okay without me. She had Sam, and to my knowledge, they actually loved each other.

Although, I wondered how differently things would have turned out if we had grown up in Nymyria. I wonder if she would still want to be with Sam.

I strolled out of my bedroom and headed for the library. I decided that it was a good day to curl up with some hot cider, a blanket, and a book. It was raining outside and there was nothing better to do anyway.

As soon as I stepped into the library, I saw silver hair peeking over a book that was blocking Arryn's face.

"You're back? I didn't realize you returned?" I tried not to sound too excited.

"Yes, just got back this—" He halted mid-sentence as he pulled the book from his face and took in my form.

His eyes danced around my body from my thighs to my chest, and then my unbound hair. I was suddenly too aware of how much skin I was showing.

"I'm sorry to be so indecent, I just woke up and I wasn't expecting anyone to be in here," I said in between nervous breaths as I crossed my goose-fleshed arms over my chest.

"Your hair."

"Yes, I know. It's quite a mess when it's down—"

Before I knew it, Arryn was right in front of me, twirling strands of my hair in between his fingers. "It's beautiful," he whispered. "I have never seen hair as beautiful as yours."

It was an effort to breathe as his gaze drifted from my hair to my lips. His whole aura seemed to glow bright like the sun as his fingers danced with my hair and his eyes caressed my face.

"Thank you," I replied softly.

His touch was so light that I could barely feel it.

"Would you like to go somewhere with me today?" he asked as he stepped back and suddenly my body felt too cold and too far from his.

"Where?"

"It's a surprise," he said walking towards the door.

"So many surprises lately." I couldn't help my toothy grin that formed.

He winked at me and too many butterflies were flying around in my stomach. I was sure that I was going to grow wings and turn into one.

"Get dressed and we will go."

He walked through the door and then poked his head back in. "And Amara—"

"Yes?" I questioned.

"Leave your hair like that… *if you want.* The world should see it," he smiled before slipping back out the door.

My stomach twisted and turned into knots. Not ones that you get when you're anxious or scared, but the kind you get when you are feeling too many emotions all at once. Ones you just can't control.

❀ ❀ ❀

Arryn led me through the woods for miles, but it only felt like a few steps as we talked and laughed the entire time. I was almost sad when we reached our destination.

We neared a group of trees lined up next to each other in the shape of a circle with wildflowers of all different colors crowded in the middle. I followed close behind Arryn, panting from the hike.

"Here we are." He turned around and reached out his hand to guide me to the trees. I reached for it and our fingers intertwined with each other. With our hands grasped tightly together, I glanced down and saw a few sparks of sun fly off from his hand. That golden aura around his skin seemed to glow brightly as it had any time we touched. I wasn't sure what that meant, but anytime I felt that giddiness in my stomach, he echoed it back by glowing bright like the sun.

Heat rose to my cheeks and I flashed a smile to him. I felt sick to my stomach but in the best way possible.

I let go of his hand to walk up ahead as he stopped at the edge of the tree line. I stood in the middle of the circle and spun around, taking in the tall trees with white blossoms. Wind began to pick up, the howl was like a harmony of instruments that sang into my ears. Each gust of wind was a different instrument that played the same melody. It seemed to be a symphony that played just for us.

"This—this is incredible." I giggled and kept spinning until I was facing Arryn again. My feet came to an abrupt halt and my eyes focused on his face.

In the past few weeks that I had known him, I had never seen him with a smile so wide as he gazed at me. Which was surprising since he had pretty much *always* been smiling unless his brother was mentioned. That was the only time I had seen him frown.

His eyes also seemed to be grinning along with his mouth, and, once again, a few drops of sunlight sparked out from his aura.

"What?" I said breaking from my laughter. My chest heaved up and down from excitement.

"Nothing." He let out a soft chuckle.

"What? Tell me!" I pressed again.

"You just look so beautiful when you're laughing." His eyes were cast over with a warmth I had not seen in him before. He angled his head down and looked up at me through raised brows.

My stomach twisted at his words, and my heart felt like it had grown wings and it was going to soar out of my body.

The feeling was foreign to me, and I wasn't sure it was one I should have been feeling.

I should have left, I should have never taken him up on his offer to live with him. I should have left when I found out his lies…. but what I *should* have done was a lot different than what I *wanted* to do.

And in that moment, I wanted nothing else than to be in his presence.

"You look good too when you smile!" I giggled and continued spinning in a circle with my arms stretched out and my head thrown back, soaking up the songs of the trees, not caring that my response sounded as if it was crafted by a child.

It was only fitting as I felt like I had morphed into that ten-year-old girl again. I felt like the world was my playground and my only objective was to *live*. Everything felt new and exciting like I was in a continuous daydream.

That little girl who dreamed of *more*, was the one spinning and listening to the sounds of the trees. She was the one laughing and giggling, living in the moment. That was for her.

He let out a hard chuckle and ran up towards me placing a hand over my back as he began to spin with me. He placed his other arm on my waist and pulled my groin in towards him, our chests inches from each other.

We kept spinning, but now it wasn't due to our feet moving under us. I looked around, and we were floating. Whirling round and round, flecks of gold swarmed us and twirled around our spinning bodies in the opposite direction.

I peeked around his shoulder to see those wings formed from vines poking out from his back. They carried us higher and higher as the music crescendoed.

I stopped laughing as my eyes met his. His breathing became sharper and the rise and fall of his chest told me everything I needed to know.

He felt it too. The sickness I had felt earlier in my stomach when our hands interlocked, and what I had felt that morning in the library.

That feeling, I didn't have with Mason, or anyone else for that matter. Mason was a chore. I knew deep down that we could never be happy together. I may have been matched to him because of his attraction to me, but my soul was never meant to be matched with his. He made that very clear.

My heart struggled to pump the blood that flowed to it, the beats increasing in pace the longer I stared into his eyes.

I am so screwed.

I knew it was a bad idea. A fate and a human?

Everything could go wrong. It was a disaster waiting to happen, but even knowing this, I didn't seem to care.

I didn't care that he would live forever and that I would just be a tiny moment in his infinite existence.

None of that mattered as for the very first time in my life, I could only see light.

Golden, bright, and welcoming light.

I couldn't control my eyelids as they blinked profusely. My hands rested on Arryn's chest as he used his magic to whirl us around faster and then suddenly let us drop, almost plummeting to the ground before he caught us again.

My laughter returned at the sudden drop in my stomach. He mimicked my laughter as he brought our feet to touch the ground again.

My hands glided down his chest before sliding down his torso and then returning to my sides. "Thank you, that was fun." I smiled. "I never had fun like this underground. I feel so…" I sucked in a deep breath through my nose and exhaled. "*Alive.*"

"I haven't either. Magic isn't new to me but with you… you make it feel as if I am experiencing it all for the first time," he sighed. "It is easy to take it all for granted when you have never lived another way."

"And it's easy to ignore the things that you don't understand. Easy to deem it as evil just because you have never experienced it before."

At that moment, I realized how truly wrong we had been. Everyone underground, if they knew what life was like above, they would never want to go back. I hadn't considered what it could be like to live above.

When you don't know something exists, you aren't capable of longing for it, but somehow I did. I longed for this feeling my entire life even though I had no idea how it could exist.

I think something deep inside of me always knew that wasn't all there was to the world. Some part of me knew there had to be something more. That magic did exist. Not just the magic the fates have, but the magic of life. *Living.* Feeling alive was the true magic.

He nodded and touched his hand to cup my cheek once before we walked off back toward the castle.

I felt new. Things that seemed to be wrong before now felt so right.

19

I couldn't stop smiling. I felt like an absolute fool. It had been a few weeks since Arryn took me to the *"Singing Aborum."*

He had told me later that is what the musical trees were called, and I still blushed at the thought of our moment together.

I pressed my hand to my cheek, imitating his final touch to me before we left.

Since that day, I hadn't seen him much as he had duties to fulfill around the castle, and political affairs to tend to. When I did see him, we would read together until we fell asleep in our chairs, or we would talk at dinner with Caris.

Caris was busy too, so most of the time I would find ways to entertain myself. I made sure never to leave the castle alone though as Arryn ordered. As much as I wanted to explore this new world, I didn't want to go behind his back.

He said that Keiran was most likely prowling along the border, waiting for me. Waiting for the perfect time to take me away. I asked Arryn why Keiran hadn't tried anything yet or attacked the Light Kingdom. Besides the enchantment over me, he had no reason to fulfill his end of the bargain now that Arryn refused to turn me over.

Arryn said that knowing Keiran, he was waiting for the time it would do the most damage.

"Amara!" Caris screamed from the kitchen. "Breakfast is ready!"

I rolled out of bed and wiped the sleep out of my eyes as I made my way downstairs. "Morning Caris." I took my seat at the table and saw that Arryn's chair had been empty. "Where is Arryn?"

"Oh, he won't be joining us. He left early this morning to attempt to meet with his brother." She said as she put my plate in front of me. I could tell it was taking all of her strength to attempt to look calm.

My throat bobbed at her words, and I couldn't help from letting the worry set in. My stomach twisted into knots so tight I wasn't sure I was going to be able to eat my breakfast. "Will he be okay?"

She sat down at the table with her plate and pursed her lips as she let out a sigh. "I hope so. I'd like to believe that Keiran wouldn't hurt him, but after last time..." She stabbed a piece of egg with her fork. "I don't put anything past Keiran." My face dropped and I could feel my skin turn green. She noticed and she shifted her whole demeanor. "You don't have to worry though! Arryn knows how to reason with him and he can protect himself."

"I hope so," I muttered.

I wished that he told me he was going to meet with Keiran, especially since it was about me. Caris didn't have to say why they were meeting, I already knew.

Caris lifted an eyebrow and let a smirk grow on her face. "You know, I had never seen Arryn that happy in my life. The day you guys came back from the trees... he was quite literally glowing," she said with a mouth full of food.

My stomach knots twisted again, but not in a bad way this time. "Well, that is part of his magic, isn't it? The glowing? And the specks of sun that fly out of him." I pushed the food around on my plate.

She stopped chewing and her eyes grew wide. "Wait. You have seen him glow... more than once? And you... saw light *fly* off of him?"

"Yes? Isn't that part of his magic?" I said confused.

"Oh, by the Threads of Fate. He didn't tell you?" She laughed. "I mean, of course, he didn't tell you. That would be extremely embarrassing."

"Tell me what?"

"I shouldn't be telling you this, but I trust you won't taunt him with this information." She pointed her fork at me as if it was a threat.

I shot my hands up and shook my head to make it clear I wouldn't say a word.

"Well…" she said hesitantly. "Arryn glows when his heartbeat accelerates. When we were little kids and he would see the girls he took a liking to, he would glow. Kids made fun of him for it, but I never did. I thought it was amazing."

My heart beat against my chest and my whole world slowed.

"Girls he took a liking to."

If he glowed around me, did that mean he…

"I didn't realize you have known each other that long," I cut in.

"Oh yes, we have been friends since we were little fates. It all started when we were in school, learning how to wield our magic. We were eating lunch, and I switched out his beans for maggots. The rest is history," she laughed.

I chuckled at the thought of him going to take a bite of his lunch and seeing maggots instead. I would pay anything to see that happen to him now.

"And what does it mean when the flecks fly off of him?" I asked as I remembered the point of this conversation.

"Well... you see, it—uh" She closed her eyes as if she was the one who was supposed to be embarrassed. "The glowing means his heart is beating faster... And the flecks of sun- You know what? I will just let Arryn tell you!"

"Oh," I replied in a high-pitched tone. I acted unfazed on the outside when really a warmth had spread through me.

🌹 🌹 🌹

It was late when I finally got to bed. Caris and I had been talking all day, sharing stories and having laughs. We may have had a few drinks too.

She told me more stories from her childhood and about Arryn when he was young. I felt giddy inside and perked up anytime she mentioned his name.

There was one point though where she was recalling a memory of him getting her the worst birthday gift ever, a shovel.

She had said *"fifty years ago, on my birthday—"* and it immediately sent me into a spiral, lost in my thoughts.

Fifty years ago?

I had stopped listening and all I could think about was how I was just a blip in their world. In *Arryn's* world.

The feelings from the day at the trees resurfaced, but this time I couldn't push them away as fast.

It didn't matter what feelings I had towards Arryn because one day, I would be dead and he would be alive. My mortal years on this earth were as simple as one hundred birthdays, if I was lucky, out of their infinity. I was a blink of an eye in their never-ending universe.

I managed to pull myself out of the hole I had dug in my mind and tried to continue on so I didn't ruin the night.

I knew she sensed I was acting odd, but she didn't say anything about it. Somehow I managed to leave those thoughts in the corner of my mind.

It was refreshing to talk to another girl.

I had one true friend underground, Poppy. As much as I loved her, and she was a good friend to me, we never had any moments like this.

None where we could just be carefree and talk about the things that made us women.

To be fair, that's not how life worked underground. Nobody did those things.

We sat together at lunch and helped each other with classwork. I spoke with her daily, and she would talk with me about Sam, but that was the extent of it.

Caris, on the other hand, I felt as if I had gotten closer to her the past month than I had ever gotten to Poppy in the twenty years I had known her.

It hurt to admit, and my stomach turned with guilt. Nothing could ever make me not love Poppy. I missed her so much, but so many things that I thought made us close were really just surface-level.

When we decided to call it a night, I was sad to leave her. I was truly exhausted, and a little wasted, but I could've talked to Caris all night and had fun.

I tucked myself into bed and rolled over to finish the book that Caris recommended to me. I only got a few pages in when I felt my eyes become so heavy that I couldn't keep them open for a second longer.

20

As soon as I heard the front door open, I ran out from the kitchen and into the entryway. I had been waiting at the dining room table, waiting for the front door to click open. Arryn was finally back from his meeting with Keiran.

As soon as I saw him, I decided not to ask right away how the meeting went. His light and his innate goodness made me blind to my selfish need to always be in the loop. I had accepted that Arryn would tell me on his own, when the time was right and when he was comfortable to do so.

"You're back!" Caris screamed running down the stairs.

"Yes, I'm back," he said with a grave expression. Then, he noticed me walking in to greet him. His golden eyes glimmered with an emotion I couldn't quite place.

"Welcome back." I dipped my head slowly and brought my eyes up to meet his.

He dipped his back in response then turned back to Caris. "We need to discuss the details of the meeting. I'll meet you in the office."

She grunted. "Now? You just got back, and you want to get back to work right away?"

He raised his eyebrows and hardened his stare and then she sighed as she made her way to the office.

He directed his gaze back to mine. "How are you?"

"Good. Bored, but I'm good," I replied.

"Bored? Don't you have those... books to keep you entertained?" He winked.

"Funny," I said as I punched him in the arm.

He let out a roar of laughter and then grabbed my fist and held it to his chest. "Or are you bored because you missed me?"

My eyes rolled so far they could've fallen out of my head. "Don't flatter yourself," I said as I ripped my arm back to my side. I turned and headed back up the stairs, still aware of him watching me. I had been wearing a silk pale green night dress that stopped at the apex of my thigh.

When I reached the top of the stairs, I glanced back to see those golden sparks of light fly out from his form. My lips curled upward into a wicked grin as I turned back around and headed into my bedroom.

❁ ❁ ❁

I remained in my bedroom waiting for them to finish their meeting. For a moment, I debated on listening in, or complaining that I wasn't invited to discuss.

It was probably boring anyway. I convinced myself.

I wondered why they couldn't discuss it in front of me. I chalked it up to Arryn wanting to tell me alone.

I hoped that was what it was. Maybe it went so poorly that he didn't want to scare me.

In the meantime, I washed and dressed for the day. I threw on a pale pink dress with white mesh sleeves that puffed at the shoulder. I braided my dark hair and then threw it to the side over my shoulder.

When I heard footsteps outside my door I knew that they were finally done. Excitement poured out of me as I flung open my door and raced down the stairs. I had been smiling so wide, ready to finally spend some time with Arryn.

When I got to the kitchen he had opened the front door and slammed it after himself.

I stopped in my tracks as I paused for a moment stunned that he would just leave like that. I was about to turn and head back to my room. But then I decided I wouldn't let him go through whatever was angering him alone.

I followed behind and ran outside, passing the rose garden as I cleared the yard. "Arryn!" I called out.

"Go back inside, Amara," he said as he continued stomping towards the woods.

My heart sank at his tone that had no ounce of compassion in it. It reminded me of how cold he had been the day Keiran first showed up, the day Caris took me to the cottage. He was so shook up.

But this, this was almost worse. This time, however, it hurt. It hurt to be shut out by him when I thought we had moved past that.

"Arryn? I'm not going back inside. I want you to talk to me! What's wrong?" I shouted as I still trailed behind him.

He stopped and spun around allowing me to close the gap between us. "You, Amara. You are what's wrong," he spat.

His words hit me like metal bouncing off metal. It rippled through my whole body.

I could feel my heart crack as it split in two. In the month that I had been there, he never spoke to me that way. He had always treated me with kindness.

"Fine. If you want to be alone, you can be alone. I don't care." I turned to leave and then felt warmth surround my arm. He grabbed just above my elbow and turned me back around to face him. His arms rested on both of my biceps, grasping tightly as he hung his head down.

"I'm sorry. I didn't mean that." He met my gaze and cupped my cheek as if his magical touch was supposed to make the anger fade.

As much as I tried to fight it, the anger flowed out from me, an anxious warmth left in its place.

"I can't protect you," he said hoarsely. "I can't protect you from *him*."

My heart began to mend as I realized he wasn't upset *at me*. He was upset because he felt like he was going to fail me.

"You don't need to worry about me. Don't let it consume you at least." I rested my hand on top of his chest. "Just live. Do what makes you happy, don't think about things that might happen… or things that haven't happened yet. Just live for now."

My lips pursed as I realized how dumb I probably sounded trying to console an immortal being who had been alive two hundred years longer than I had. He didn't need my advice.

"You're right." His gaze flashed back and forth between my eyes. "I need to do what makes me happy."

"And what makes you happy?" I said in a breathy voice, feeling my chest rise and fall faster with each second that passed.

He smiled and directed his line of site to my lips. He brought his other hand to the back of my neck, the other still cupping my cheek.

"This," he whispered as he pulled me in, his lips meeting mine gently.

Our lips interlocked and danced between each other. Our rhythm synced and the gentle kisses became more passionate. *Deeper.* I felt like I couldn't get enough of his taste. That his kisses wouldn't be enough soon.

Specks of light flew from him and danced between our lips each time we pulled away to take in the sight of each other before diving back in.

The light stuck to my lips and body, exuding a warmth that felt as if the sun was cradling me.

That kiss— It was a long time coming. Everything between us had been building up to that moment.

"Well, I am glad you could cheer him up!" Caris shouted out the door from inside the castle. The sounds of her giggles resonated and bounced off the trees behind us as we broke apart from each other. His hand was still on the back of my neck, and he smiled as he faced toward the castle.

"Thank you for that Caris!" he replied.

"Anytime! Dinner is ready, whenever you guys are done… with *that*." She shut the door.

My tongue swept across my bottom lip as I sheepishly grinned at him. His hand traced down my lower back and stopped in the middle, guiding me forward back to the castle. He glanced over to look at me as we walked towards it.

That look.

Those golden eyes. They spoke to me, to my soul. My heart beat so fast like it was going to explode any second.

If he kept looking at me that way, it would have.

🌹 🌹 🌹

The entire dinner I couldn't stop staring at Arryn and every time he met my gaze with his, a heat welled up in my chest that tempted to make its way down.

"You two are going to have to stop with the eyes. And please, for the love of fate, can you *try* to calm yourselves down?" Caris stabbed a leafy green with her fork. "I can *smell* you from over here."

Smell us? I guess it made sense that if the fates had enhanced hearing and speed then they would have a heightened sense of smell too.

My face went flushed and I felt embarrassment paint itself over my cheeks. "Sorry," I said.

"It's not so much you as it is Arryn." She threw him a disgusted glance. "Please, just think about the food in front of you instead before you start sparking everywhere."

I snorted and then turned my attention to the plate in front of me, making sure not to look at Arryn again.

21

The darkness swirled around me and then blew forward. It was begging me to follow it. As much as I knew I shouldn't, my feet disobeyed. They chased after the darkness that seemed to lead further into the night. Leading me farther away from daylight and into the night sky. The darkness stopped and then took form, an open hand appearing in front of me. It uncurled as if it was asking for me to take it. I reluctantly placed my hand into it, and then it curled around mine tightly. The rest of the darkness began to solidify past the hand forming a shoulder, then a neck, a body, and then a head. One that I recognized.

    I screamed.

I tried to let go and back away from him, but the hand only held on tighter. It wouldn't let go no matter how hard I tried to escape.

That wicked smile formed on his face. His black eyes turned silver at my struggle. He laughed at me and then yanked on my arm, pulling my body closer to his.

"Please, let me go," I begged him. "Please, Keiran."

He laughed and then licked his bottom lip.

"But this..." His eyes looked up and his head cocked to the side as if he was looking at someone. "Is so much more fun." He gripped the bottom of my chin before I could turn around. It was as if he had sucked the fear out of me and put me under some sort of spell. I found myself leaning into his chest. My lips were mere inches from his.

Suddenly, inky black darkness poured out from my mouth and spilled onto the ground below us. Keiran was laughing and leaned in even closer.

I was choking. Choking on the darkness—

"Amara!" I heard a familiar voice in the background. It was calling out to me, begging me-

"AMARA!"

I awoke to Arryn above me, his hands gripped on either of my shoulders. His chest heaving.

"Amara, are you okay?"

I was drenched in sweat, my throat sore as if I had been screaming my lungs out.

"What happened?" I panted.

"You were screaming. I heard you all the way down the hall, you were begging for help and you said Keiran's name. I thought—" He paused to let

out a heavy breath. "I thought he might have come to take you, so I hurried in here, but it was just a nightmare," Arryn said caressing the side of my cheek with the back of his hand.

"I'm sorry for waking you," I said. My voice was extremely hoarse. I reached to grab the glass of water near my bed and Arryn was there in an instant, picking it up for me.

He slipped one hand under my head to lift me and the other brought the glass slowly to my lips.

His touch was gentle and nothing like the touch from my nightmare. Keiran was the opposite of kind. His actions were spiteful and filled with rage.

"Thank you," I said, resting my head back on the pillow.

"I'm glad you're alright," Arryn said and I knew that he meant it from the worried look in his eyes when I first woke up.

He turned to make his way out.

"Wait—" I said and he paused. "Will you... stay with me?"

He faced me again and I could see his breathing hitch. "Of course," he breathed.

I peeled back the covers next to me and patted the empty spot with my hand. Hopefully, he would think the action was charming rather than awkward.

He slid under the covers and it was then that I realized he had not been wearing a shirt.

Arryn lay on his back with his arms crossed over his chest.

"Can you hold me?" I whispered.

Without a second thought, Arryn turned over onto his side and wrapped his arms around me. He pulled me closer to him, my back pressed against his chest. His skin against mine was like silk against satin, a smooth and sensuous encounter that sent shivers of pleasure down my spine.

His warmth enveloped me and made my entire body fall in relaxation. I hadn't realized how tense I was until he was holding me.

His breath was hot against my neck. I felt every exhale and knew exactly how long it would be before the next one would come.

I took in a deep inhale of his scent. He smelled of dandelions and honey with a touch of sandalwood.

Arryn leaned his head in and pressed a soft kiss to the back of my neck. The movement was intended to be sweet, but it instantly set my nerves on fire.

He pulled me even closer, our legs interlocking.

I was so comfortable. More comfortable than I had ever been in my whole life. Everything felt *calm.* So calm that before I knew it, the night had claimed me despite my desires.

22

Arryn wasn't next to me when I woke up. For a second I thought that I had dreamt our whole encounter, but then he waltzed in, a teacup in his hand.

"I figured you would want to rest today since your sleep was interrupted last night," he said handing me the cup. It smelled of mint and honey.

"Thank you, but I'm fine. I have nightmares a lot. It's nothing new to me." I said taking a long sip of the tea.

He thought for a moment before plopping onto the edge of my bed. "I don't want your dreams to be plagued by him. I wish there was something I could do—"

"Arryn, *I am fine*," I responded, reaching to touch his knee. I knew he needed comforting more than I did at that moment.

He thought it was his fault that I was having nightmares, but he had no idea how long I had been plagued by them.

It was true that Keiran had never been in them before, but I would've had a nightmare regardless.

His silver hair fell in front of his eyes as he brought his head down. He inhaled and when his gaze met mine, his worried expression was completely wiped from his face. "Okay, I will have to take your word on it, but you should rest today."

"I was actually hoping that we could go somewhere. Or just get out of the house?"

Arryn was quiet for a few moments and then stood as if he was going to leave. "I have just the place. Meet me downstairs in thirty minutes."

"Where are we going?" I laughed as he pranced out of my bedroom.

He turned back only to flash that cheeky smile at me, one that always sent my heart beating noticeably faster, before he slipped through the doorway without another word.

Hurrying off the bed, I stumbled to the closet and shuffled through my clothes. I decided on one dress in particular that I knew would drive him wild.

It was a white dress crafted from the softest silk and cinched at the waist with a golden ribbon. The straps were mesh with green vines sewn into them. It looked as if vines were holding the dress up.

My hair was down, but I decided to tie a few strands back with a green bow that I found in the dresser which matched the vines on the dress.

I raced down the stairs to find Arryn waiting by the door, a blanket and a picnic basket in his hands.

He almost dropped the basket when he saw me, his cheeks turned a pinkish hue. With eyes wide, he cleared his throat and then reached his arm out for me to hold. "Shall we?"

I wrapped my arm around his and our eyes met before we turned to walk outside.

"You look beautiful, Amara." His eyes roamed around my face as if he was memorizing my every feature, every freckle on my face, every speck of color in my eyes.

I smiled and looked to the ground, my cheeks turning crimson. His fingers gently touched the bottom of my chin and tilted my head back up to meet his gaze.

"You're beautiful," he repeated.

As hard as it was for me to feel beautiful after never feeling like I was enough underground, I believed him. I believed that he did look at me and see beauty, even though I couldn't do it for myself sometimes.

🌹 🌹 🌹

I sprawled out onto the blanket that Arryn had laid down on the grass. My hair swept over my face because of the wind and my hands held my dress down at my sides to keep it from blowing up.

Arryn had taken me to a grassy knoll near the castle. White flowers were surrounding us that hadn't seemed to bloom yet, but I was sure they would be exquisite.

The emerald green grass was tall around us, and butterflies and bumble bees flew from flower to flower.

We rolled around in the grass talking and looking up at the sky for hours, and then we watched the clouds and saw them morph from bunnies to fairies, trees, and frogs. Anything our minds could imagine.

"That one…" Arryn said with a hand resting under the back of his head while the other lay at his side. "Looks a lot like a heart."

"Hmm… it's either that or a plump backside." I turned my head so that I was facing Arryn.

He burst out into laughter before turning his face to mine. "You've got a quite mischievous mind, Amara. But, yes… now that you say that it *does* look more like that."

"I like your idea better," I said tucking my hands underneath the side of my head.

"Oh, yeah?"

"Yeah," I muttered.

He slid his hand over my chest and onto my heart. "Yours is beating... quite fast." His words staggered.

I audibly gulped and then reached my hand to his heart, my fingers tracing circles over his shirt. "So is yours."

I internally took pleasure in the fact his heart was beating even faster than mine. It was practically pounding out of his chest, and I wasn't sure how it had stayed inside.

"Tell me this is real. Tell me I am not dreaming," I whispered to him, my gaze set on his mouth.

An emotion I wasn't sure of passed over his face quickly before a smile took over. "This is real— He brought his mouth to mine, and his warm lips interlocked with mine in a sweet gentle kiss before he pulled back a few inches so that he could look into my eyes. "And you're not dreaming."

As his lips met mine once more, my heart danced and my spirit soared. I felt as if I was flying and then suddenly dropped out of the sky only to be caught and swept up by the wind.

When he finally pulled back, he wrapped his arm around my shoulder. I rested my head on his chest, and we continued staring up at the sky.

This.
I could do this forever.

23

We stayed in the grass on that blanket for hours.

So long that the sun began to set over the green mountains in front of us. The sky was painted in hues of vibrant orange, yellow, and soft pink.

At that moment, it occurred to me that I had never actually seen a sunset. I had been there for a month and I had seen the daytime and nighttime, but never a sunset.

As it grew darker, I noticed the flowers around us had begun to bloom. The white flowers that had been closed when we arrived were almost fully open.

"Arryn, look!" I said pointing to them. "They were closed this morning." I looked at him and his face was as if he had been waiting for me to notice.

"They are moonlight flowers. The bloom only at night. Then the petals fall and new ones replace them by morning. The whole process happens again, night after night." His grin sent a warmth shooting through my veins.

It was fully night time and the petals of the moonlight flowers began to glow. The glow was not of the moon but resembled the sun.

"Ironic that they glow like sunlight but are called moonlight flowers." I turned my head, glancing back at him over my shoulder.

"Yes. The name sunlight flowers *would* fit their glow better, but they only come out in the *moonlight*. The moonlight is really what triggers their bloom," he responded gently.

"Amazing," I breathed.

The glowing petals then began falling off of the flowers, one by one. Instead of falling to the ground, they began floating up to the sky, towards the moonlight.

"And there's that—also why they are called moonlight flowers," he said in a coy manner.

Unable to speak or form any words that would even begin to explain how beautiful the sight was, I laid down on the blanket, watching the petals float up to the moon as if they were lightning bugs in an open field. These, however, were far more spectacular.

One of the petals floated above me, and I reached out for it. Gold painted my fingertips before it flew up into the night sky.

Arryn took his place beside me, his arm to his side.

My arm was next to my side too. Our hands almost touching.

His pinkie curled up closer to mine before reaching out slowly to uncurl my hand into his.

For some reason, this small action had my heart leaping and fluttering. It felt far more intimate than a kiss.

A kiss was attraction, but holding hands? That was something *more*. It meant something more.

What did it mean for us?

Without thinking about it further, I pulled his hand over my stomach and dragged it slowly down to my thigh.

Every nerve in my body vibrated as I made what I wanted very clear.

"Amara—are you sure?" he questioned as I pulled it lower.

"Yes," I replied softly.

Without a second thought, Arryn moved and before I could blink he was atop me.

"You don't know how long I've wanted to do this," he said between ragged breaths.

"Then do it," I panted. Our mouths were so close I could feel his hot breath against my lips.

In a swift motion, his lips met with mine. His hand moved up my back, warmth trailing in its wake as it moved higher toward the zipper.

"Amara..."

The way he said my name—it was as if it was the answer to all his prayers.

"Please," I begged, not quite sure *what* I was begging for.

Just then, I felt his vines crawl out from his wrists. They traveled down my sides before reaching my legs and wrapping around my thighs.

Gold sparks poured out from Arryn as his vines moved further.

❁ ❁ ❁

Arryn and I had spent the whole night tangled up in each other. We spent only *half* of the night sleeping.

We only decided to leave when the darkness turned into daylight, and it was then that I realized that I had never seen a sunrise either.

The sunset had been beautiful, but the sun rising over the tall trees and the way the world felt so still and quiet beforehand... like the world was empty and the only ones who lived in it were Arryn and I.

The way the magic in the kingdom seemed to *awaken* with the rising sun, was like nothing else.

It seemed fitting that Arryn and I had become one as the dawn broke. An awakening of some sort... not just for the world, but for my heart.

I was so blind underground. Not just to the outside world, but to my feelings.

All those years I spent yearning to be somewhere else... I think maybe somehow I knew that I was supposed to be here.

For years I dreamed of the sun and its warmth. What it would feel like.

And now, when I look at Arryn and I see the gold light in his eyes, I know that he is the light I was waiting for.

24

"We have to do something. I can't just sit around any longer waiting for him to attack," Arryn grumbled as he dropped his fork onto his plate. The sound reverberated through the dining room.

The past few days with Arryn have been everything I didn't know I could have. From shopping, reading by the fire, and the moments where we were tangled up in the sheets together had been amazing.

However, the bliss came to a sudden halt that morning when Caris went outside to tend to the garden and found the castle had gone from its usually bright white color that seemed to glow, to pitch black.

It was as if darkness itself had clung to the iridescent paint. Caris tried to scrub it off, but it wouldn't budge. The only way for it to come off was for Arryn to use a blast of his sun magic to cancel out the darkness that surrounded it.

When Caris ran into the castle sobbing, I knew it was bad, but it was even worse than Arryn and I had expected.

"This was a warning. He can get into our lands with no problem and do something like this without any of us noticing. He isn't going to stop, so we need to put an end to it. Now." I wasn't sure who was speaking, because it wasn't the Arryn I had been spending my days with. His voice didn't have that playful vibrant quality anymore. It was somber and demanding. I hated the effect that Keiran had on him.

I *hated* Keiran.

"What do we do?" I asked with a nervous tremor in my voice.

Arryn and Caris both looked at me before swapping glances with each other.

"We… need to trick him into coming out of wherever he's hiding. Bait him…" Caris said looking between the two of us with implications.

Arryn clenched his fist together until his knuckles turned white, "No. We are not going to use her-"

"I'll do it," I interrupted.

Their expressions shifted to surprise as they both turned their attention toward me.

"No, Amara," Arryn said as he looked at me with furrowed brows. "End of story."

End of story?

"Fine," I said leaning back into my chair with crossed arms.

Arryn's tone lightened as he grabbed my hand in his. "We will figure out another way... *Another way.*" He repeated the last part as glared at Caris.

"Another way," She agreed. "Sorry for even mentioning it. That was a stupid idea... What about the witches? We could ask them for help?"

Arryn grimaced, "We can't trust them. They are just as evil as dark fates and as dangerous, if not more, than a soul reaper."

I shuddered at the thought of a being more dangerous than a soul reaper.

"Don't you have armies? Can't you just send them in to attack him?" I asked.

"I could, but the problem is that he too has armies — ones that are probably more powerful and stronger in numbers. If I send my armies in to attack the Dark Kingdom, his would retaliate and come back twice as strong," He replied.

"Right..." I felt dumb for even asking. It seemed so obvious now that he laid it out for me, and now I was even more confused about what we should do.

"What are we going to do?" I said softly as if I was whispering to myself.

Arryn dropped his head down and then stood up. "I need to think," he said as he walked out of the office and closed the door behind him.

While he was thinking, so was I.

❁ ❁ ❁

I came up behind Arryn, pressing a kiss to his shoulder and squeezing his arms with my hands.

He groaned at my touch before turning around to press his mouth to my forehead.

"When this is all over… I want to help the humans," I finally said. He still hadn't come up with a plan, at least we hadn't talked about it since the meeting earlier.

He tensed and then pulled back to see my entire face.

"I love that you want to help them… But I told you, they didn't want help before, they won't want it now." He cupped his hand around my cheek.

"We have to do something. At least give those who don't know what it's like up here an option to live above," I pleaded.

I tried not to think about those I left behind underground. At first, if felt like I was the one who was going to suffer, but now I felt as if they were the ones who were trapped. Banished to live underground for their whole lives.

I thought of my mother and Poppy. I wondered if they thought about me... if they missed me like I did them.

I knew Poppy most likely did, but I wasn't so sure about my mother.

His smile faded and his eyes glazed over as if he was debating something.

"What is it?" I asked.

"Nothing." The smile returned, but his eyes didn't match it. "We can talk about it later. After everything, if- *When* it all goes well." He pulled me into a hug. As much as I wanted to fall into it and let his touch consume me, I couldn't help but feel like there was something he wasn't telling me.

I never had a gut feeling that *wasn't* correct, but in that moment I clung to the hope that I *was* wrong.

I knew the blush was visible on my face as I imagined living out the rest of my days with Arryn, but then worry spread through my nerves as I remembered the biggest difference between us. He would be there long after I am gone.

Swallowing my fear, I chose to ignore that gut feeling, to choose Arryn. I doubted he would lie to me again after the last time.

Things are different now. I told myself.

We didn't have the same relationship before. We didn't even *have* a relationship before. He wouldn't lie to me now.

I kissed him and then pulled him over to my bed.

"Later. We can talk later." I agreed.

I squealed as he tossed me onto the bed and began pressing kisses along my entire body.
Later.

25

Arryn pulled me into his side, nestling his head into my neck as he breathed in my scent like it was his last dying breath. I couldn't stop the flutter of my heart and the shiver that coursed through my body.

"Say the word, and we can run away together," he said stroking my hair. "We can go live off the land and get away from Keiran. I will give up being king."

I inhaled slowly and then rested my head against his. "As tempting as that sounds… We can't leave these people in Keiran's hands."

"I know," he admitted as his eyes met mine with reluctance, but then his arm slid around my waist, pulling me closer. "It was nice to dream about it for a moment though. Leaving this all behind…"

He tucked my hair behind my ear, "Spending my days with you… doing *whatever. We. Want.* "

It took all my strength to pull away from him. "Promise that when you get back we will live out those dreams of yours?" I bit my lip and batted my eyelashes.

He smiled as he pulled me flesh up against his body. "Oh, we will do all that and *more*," He promised.

I giggled as he pressed a kiss to my cheek and then headed out. He was going to meet with the commanders of his armies to help form a plan. We hadn't gotten anywhere in the past few days by ourselves, and our worries only grew stronger.

Wondering what Keiran was planning and what his next move was took over all of our minds, even if we didn't admit it to each other.

I peered out from my balcony as I watched Arryn's vines stretch out across his back before he flew into the air.

The smile on my face dropped, and as soon as he was out of sight, I raced down the stairs of the castle on quiet toes, making sure no one saw or heard me.

I passed a few of the maids when I left my room, but they just smiled at me as I pretended to go into the library. When they were gone, I made a run for the front gate.

I pulled the door open and closed it just as fast after my body cleared through the opening.

The autumn air nipped at my skin with its cold chill. A sign that I should return inside, but I didn't.

❀ ❀ ❀

I reached the border that divided the two kingdoms. The glow in the air and speckles of light that floated through the air in the Light Kingdom, as if they were drops from the sun, stopped at the border.

The air was clear past it. No light danced through it, and there was no warm glow beyond the border. It was strange to see how suddenly it changed as if there were some invisible line dividing the lands.

I walked along the side of the border, sticking my hand through the invisible line and letting my scent drift across.

I walked alone down the border for what felt like an eternity. I decided it was then time for the second part of my plan. I pulled out a knife I had brought with me and made a small incision in my hand.

I figured that if he had already tasted my blood for enjoyment, then another taste might draw him out.

Wincing, I squeezed out drops of blood from my hand as I continued walking.

I felt his presence before I saw him.

A cold gust of wind seemed to caress my neck, sliding around my head and then down my back. It surrounded my entire body in what felt like a light touch from freezing hands.

The ground became overshadowed as if a storm cloud rolled over, completely covering any light from the sun.

My heart practically stopped and my gut feeling told me someone was right there. That voice in my head, however, didn't tell me to run. It was quiet, almost as if it was silently urging me to *look*.

I hesitantly made a half turn, and my body froze when I beheld the black-clothed man standing before me. His tousled and middle-parted silk-black hair swooped down both sides of his head and stopped just above his slightly pointed ears. A few strands in the front fell over his forehead. His black eyes pierced into me as if they could see into my very soul.

Silver accents and embellishments complemented the black of his clothes. It was the same way that silver appeared around his irises the last time I had seen him.

Seeing him in the sunlight instead of darkness was much different. I had barely been able to see his face in the art shop, besides basic shapes and his glowing eyes.

When our gazes met, I knew I messed up. I shouldn't have tried to deal with this without Arryn or Caris, but I felt like I could lure him in. Maybe he would try to take me and then the enchantment would turn him to stone long enough for Arryn to get back and deal with him.

As I beheld Keiran, I now realized my plan was not well thought out.

As much as I knew I had to try to stop him, I couldn't help the swirl in my stomach that told me I was making a huge mistake for coming alone.

Too late now.

"Did you come here just to stare at me? I know all about your deal with Arryn. I know how pathetic you are for sending your brother to do all your dirty work," I snapped at him.

He said nothing. His mouth barely quirked up into a half-smile as his head cocked to the side and his eyes squinted slightly. His irises were now fully black as they seemed to look through my skin and into my soul.

The feeling he gave me was similar to how the soul reaper made me feel. It was like he was empty behind those dark eyes. *Numb.*

"What do you want with me anyway? Did you just want to torture a human girl? Use me for some demented purpose?" I asked sarcastically. "It's actually embarrassing for you. That it has taken you so long to *get* me. You would think for someone so powerful—"

"Is that really the best you can do?" His voice was so smooth it hummed as the sound carried into my ears. "Was *this* the *grand* plan? Surely you can do better than this, Arryn?" He raised his voice and looked around.

My stomach dropped. "He isn't here."

He sniffed and then snickered as he stalked closer to the border between us. "Incredible. You thought you could come here alone, and do what exactly? What are *you* going to do?"

"More than you could—"

That line between kept him from snatching me up and running. I had never been so thankful for something I couldn't see.

He gritted his teeth, but somehow, the action still felt careless, and relaxed. "Do you take me for a fool? You thought you could just upset me enough so that I foolishly take you out of anger, against your will? *Tsk, Tsk, Tsk,*" he muttered disapprovingly as he shook his head. "It will not be that easy."

My brain told me to run away, but my body told me something different. There was some imaginary force, a string pulling me towards him. I tried to pull back against it, but I couldn't.

Confusion etched itself into his face as I made a step towards him.

I listened for that voice, to tell me anything. Anything to help me.

Nothing.

My eyes were locked onto his as if I was in some trance.

He must have put a magic spell on me, or an enchantment.

My leg moved forward in another traitorous step, this time crossing over the border. If my whole body went over, then I was free game. He could take me away and there would be nothing Arryn could do about it because I wasn't in the Light Kingdom.

And because he had no idea that I was even here.

Beads of sweat lined my forehead as I fought against the urge to step towards him.

Help. Help me Arryn.

Arryn isn't here, Amara. You need to help yourself.

Pushing against that invisible thread of darkness pulling me towards him, I grunted. Suddenly, my foot fell backward back into the Light Kingdom and I dropped to the ground, panting with exhaustion.

Keiran cocked his head sideways and then crouched down so that we would be at eye level. "Brave little thing, aren't you? Too bad you are stifling yourself with trying to be *good.*"

"I am not *'trying to be good!'*" I shouted as I brought my face closer to that invisible wall that divided us. "I *am* good!"

Our faces were now only inches apart, the invisible border the only thing keeping us separated as I huffed in anger.

Keiran scoffed and then shook his head as if responding wasn't even worth his time. "Keep telling yourself that," he said as he also brought himself closer to that border.

Anger seemed to steam off my skin as I glared at him. I knew I had to try to keep my cool. All it would take was for me to accidentally cross over and he could take me away. I had to be careful.

It was a strange game that we were playing. It was almost as if we were both waiting for the other to make a mistake. I was waiting for him to take me so that he would turn to stone, and he was waiting for me to accidentally cross the border.

"You think because you're with Arryn. Because he likes *you*, that you are somehow good… Maybe you should join me? Live up to your full potential." He flashed a smile that was somehow the opposite of kind.

"I would never go anywhere with you, let alone help you." I don't know what you want from me, but just leave us alone!" I sat up on my knees to be higher than him.

"Never say never," he said, standing up fully so that he was now much taller than me. "You poor thing," his voice suggested he actually did not feel bad for me. "You have no idea, do you?"

My heart dropped at his words. If there was one thing I didn't have control over, it was my endless quest of curiosity.

I wanted to ask him what he was talking about, and just as I was about to, I heard a rustle in the bushes as a ball of sun struck forward, missing Keiran by an inch.

"Get away from her!" Arryn shouted as he grabbed my arm to pull me back further into the Light Kingdom.

As if the magic Keiran put on me awoke at Arryn's presence, I began moving toward the border again, bringing my foot once again over that invisible line.

"*Can't. Stop,*" I muttered to Arryn as I fought against the spell that moved me.

"Take the enchantment off of her Keiran. This loophole of yours is still breaking the rules. If she crosses over due to a spell that *you* put on her, you will turn to stone. And I *will* go to war on your kingdom to get her back," Arryn growled.

"Brother," Keiran ground out. "I do not have any *enchantment* on her. There is no magic spell. She is doing this by her own volition." He flashed a devilish grin as he grazed over my body with an amused look on his face.

"Liar," Arryn spat. His anger flowed out from him like flames.

"Fine, don't believe me. Either way, I don't care." His eyes moved from me before they settled on Arryn. "Tell me Arryn, have you told Amara yet? Not just about our little deal, but the real reason you don't want her to leave you *so soon*?" He drew out the syllables of the last two words in an effort to get under Arryn's skin.

I winced as I struggled to keep myself on the light side of the border, not bothering to pay any attention to Keiran's words. I didn't trust a thing he said anyway.

"Shut your damn mouth Keiran and take the spell off her!" Arryn barred his teeth as he threw another ball of light from his palm towards Keiran.

As if it took no effort at all, Keiran lifted his hand and darkness seeped out from it, enough to snuff out the light that Arryn threw. It happened so quickly that I almost missed it.

My stomach dropped as I realized just how powerful Keiran was. He reacted against Arryn's magic as if it was dust that he flicked off from him.

Darkness continued to flow towards Arryn until it wrapped around his neck tightly and he was gagging. His body was lifted into the air.

Arryn struggled to pull it off, but it was no use.

"Stop! Let him go! Please!" I managed to break out of the spell that moved me towards him. Tears rolled down my cheeks as I watched Arryn's face turn red from the loss of air. "Please! Let him go! I will do anything!"

Keiran only laughed before darkness pulled away in a flash, dropping Arryn onto the ground. I rushed over to him as he gasped over and over again.

"Don't make promises you can't keep, *little flower*... besides, I will have you one way or another. No need to betray Arryn anymore than you already have by coming here in the first place."

I scowled at Keiran but didn't respond as I was too worried about Arryn to care about his new nickname for me.

"I wonder if she will still love you when she finds out." His eyes met mine and then in a flash, his form turned to mist. A dark cloud that dissipated into the sky.

Love. The word sent a shock wave through my body, and I dropped to the ground with exhaustion from trying to fight the spell.

"Amara—" Arryn breathed as he scooped me up with both arms. "Why would you come here alone?" He repeated it over and over again as my eyes closed and my vision turned to black.

26

Arryn carried me all the way back to the castle as I dozed in and out of consciousness.

It didn't work.

Of course, it didn't work.

I thought I could take on Keiran alone.

How foolish I had been to think *that* would work against Keiran.

Now I had to explain to Arryn why I lied to him. I didn't technically lie, but I definitely went behind his back and almost got myself and him killed.

I was supposed to get Keiran angry, bait him to come out, and then rile him up enough so that he took me out of anger. If he had done that, he wouldn't have been able to move. Caris' magic of petrification that infused the enchantment would have turned him to stone.

Maybe if I had asked Caris she would have agreed to come with me. She could have gotten close enough to Keiran to look into his eyes for her magic to work.

It didn't matter, because it all went to shit anyways.

Even if I did ask Caris or consult Arryn in my plan, something tells me it wouldn't have worked either way. Keiran was just too powerful, and war strategy was something I did not understand.

How could I even think that I would be able to stop Keiran by myself?

I groaned as I felt strong arms around me. The fire blazed beside me and warmed my body.

"You're awake," Arryn sighed with relief before I saw frustration take over. "Why would you do that?"

"I don't know," I admitted softly. "I just wanted to help."

Arryn rubbed my side as his gaze darted between my eyes. "I know… but you can't go and do reckless things like that. He could have killed you, Amara. I don't know what he wants with you—"

"I'm sorry."

He sharply inhaled and then pushed my hair behind my ear. "I forgive you. I was just worried, not angry. Besides… how could I be angry at the girl who stuck her neck out for me?" He smiled. "You risked everything to save us. It was dumb, reckless, and idiotic… but—"

"Romantic?" I laughed dryly.

"Yes," he breathed before pressing his lips into mine.

He pulled back and caressed my cheek with the backs of his fingers.

"What happened anyways? Did he put some magic on me? Cast a spell?" I wanted answers for why my body reacted so strangely to him. Why I couldn't control myself from giving myself right to him?

"I don't know." Arryn shook his head. "I don't have knowledge of spells or how magic like that is even used. Raw magic, the magic that fates were born with—*spells, curses, and hexes*, those are different… a different type of ancient magic that is drawn from something else. It is not so simple as light and dark."

"Well who knows about it, who could we ask that can help us? Help *me*?" I asked with desperation.

He was quiet for a moment, reluctance swirling in his golden eyes. He ran his hand through his silver hair, messy from no doubt staying up all night to make sure I was okay. "The witches. They would know."

"Let's go see the witches then—" I made to stand up, but his arms tightened, pulling me back into him.

"We can't. It's too dangerous. They are hidden in a magical forest that plays tricks on those who wish to find them, and they're extremely hard to find. Even if we do find them, they are untrustworthy. They have been known to sell out those who seek out their services to higher payers. They will turn their backs on us in an instant if it benefits them."

I wanted to tell him how urgent this was, how the spell made Keiran's darkness seem to call to me. It drew me in like a siren song and I wasn't sure if I would be able to fight it next time.

The witches didn't scare me. Not anymore compared to the feeling I had when I thought Arryn was going to die.

"It can't be any more dangerous than what we just faced. I need to fix this. What if I willingly go with him, then I'll be gone. *Forever.* I—" My voice broke as I turned to face him. "I can't leave this place. I can't leave *you*."

"Oh, Amara." His voice came out soft as he brought his forehead to meet mine. His hand met the side of my cheek in a gentle caress. "The only way I will ever let you be taken from me is if it was *your own* choice. No spell or hex is going to take you from me. He will have to do better than that."

He pressed his lips to my forehead in a deep kiss. I felt the burn in my eyes as he continued. "We will figure this out. First thing tomorrow we will go to the witches… as much as I hate to turn to them, we have no other options left."

I perked up with excitement at the fact we would go, *together*. Mostly at the fact he was willing to risk everything to save me. To *have* me.

"How do you know about these witches anyway?" I asked as I placed my palm on his chest.

"I always heard stories about them as a child," he said flatly.

"I hope that the stories were wrong and they are actually as sweet as the sugar cherry fairies," I muttered.

Arryn let out a short chuckle. "Me too."

Something in his eyes told me he knew they would be nothing like the sugar cherry fairies, but he wanted to let me hope. He didn't want to extinguish that light in my eyes and the hope in my soul.

※ ※ ※

"Witches Cove" was what Arryn called it. The place where the witches lived beyond the dark forest that played tricks on your mind. He said that it was spelled by the witches to trick any trespassers.

"You can not trust anything that you see in the woods, or even trust your sight," he said. The best way to get through it is to keep your eyes closed and your head down. Anything could be a trick to lead you to your death.

Witches Cove was neither in the Light Kingdom, nor the Dark. It was its own place entirely.

Arryn used his fate speed to run us up to the front of the woods. "We should walk, quietly, the rest of the way," he said.

"Who are we going to meet?" I whispered as I slid out of his arms.

"Selene Darkhart," he grumbled as if it was an effort to even say her name. "I've heard she doesn't like other women... especially those who are beautiful." His mouth curled upward to a flirtatious grin. "You should be very selective with your words because she will most likely hate you the second she lays eyes on you since you *are* the most beautiful woman alive."

Even though we were so close to potential danger, my heart thumped and butterflies flew around in my stomach. I could feel my cheeks turn red and my eyes blinked too fast.

The sweet tension that lingered between us was cut short by a howl that escaped from the woods. It didn't sound like a wolf, more like a demon of some sort. Whatever it was, I knew I didn't want to run into it. Judging by Arryn's face, he didn't either.

A cold chill went up my spine as we entered the woods, and the little voice seemed to urge me to follow deeper into it.

Keep your head down. Do not look around.

Arryn squeezed my hand as he led me behind him. Every rustle of leaves and crack of twigs made me jump. I thought every sound was from some sort of creature about to attack us.

My heart was in my throat, thumping louder every step that we took deeper into the enchanted forest of darkness and tricks.

"Amara," a voice whispered as if it was right next to my ear.

"Arryn, did you hear that?" I asked him.

"Hear what?" He turned around, and what I saw made me let go of his hand and jump back several steps.

Black hair. Black eyes with silver glowing irises. A face that was so captivating, but so emotionless at the same time.

"What are *you* doing here," I spat as I backed up in fear.

His smile turned feral as he took a step towards me and gripped the sides of my arms.

I screamed and pushed him off.

"Amara…" He drew out the last syllable of my name with a whisper that echoed and caressed inside of my ears. His hands slid down my sides.

I closed my eyes as the voice filled my eardrums with a sound so sweet it was euphoric.

The sound then came to a sudden halt and then my eyelids flew open. Golden eyes stared back at me with confusion and concern swirling in them. Silver-shaggy hair replaced the violet-black hair that had been there a moment before.

Arryn.

Oh my—

Common sense flooded back to me like a brick falling into a pool of water. Anger crept up next as I realized the forest had tricked me, and I fell for it.

It also tricked my body into thinking it was enjoying itself. It was either the forest or the spell I could thank for that.

I gulped audibly. "I—the forest… it tricked me. It invaded my mind and changed my thoughts. Let's get the hell out of here."

"I was going to say the same thing," he said turning us around.

"No, Arryn, not out as in *leave*. We need to still go to the witches," I said, pulling him back.

"Fine," he sighed. "But you're getting on my back and I am going to run us out of here. I don't want to hear you say my brother's name *that way* ever again."

He said with a tenseness that he had never had when speaking to me before.

Embarrassment went straight to my cheeks. "Arryn—" I started.

"It's not your fault. I know, but we need to get out of here. I think we are better off going fast rather than quiet," he said pulling me up onto his back.

"You know it's just the forest Arryn, and the spell. I hate *him*." I practically growled the last word.

"I know, but that almost makes me even more upset. The fact you're feeling things that aren't real, that you can't control yourself… I could kill him for it," he said before taking off into a sprint.

As he began to run, I heard a scream.

"Help me! Arryn! Amara! Help!"

Arryn immediately stopped dead in his tracks and looked at me with an expression that asked *"Did you hear that too?"*

"Is that Caris?" I breathed.

"Sounded like it," he said lifting me off from his back. "Caris!" he yelled.

"Over here!" She called back.

Something like unease settled in the pit of my stomach, but I followed anyway. I wasn't sure why she followed after us after she opted to stay back at the castle.

"We're coming! Stay there!" he screamed back.

I followed Arryn deeper into the woods, the light from the moon seemed to dissipate with the more trees that hung over us.

"Over here!" she shouted again. The sound was now only a few feet away from us.

"Where are you?" I asked.

Something didn't feel right. Something was off. I didn't know what but-

"Get out."

My voice urged me to leave, furthering my suspicions.

"Arryn, I think something is wrong. I don't think she is-"

Before I could finish my sentence, I spotted a short figure standing not far from us.

"Look—" I whispered to Arryn. "What is that?"

He whipped his head around to the figure and immediately put an arm out to block me from it.

"Who are you? Are you alright?" He called out to it.

No response.

The figure took a step forward.

"Hello?" Arryn called out.

No response.

Arryn lifted his palm out and formed a small ball of sunlight. He aimed it toward the figure and I let out a scream when I observed the soggy gelatin looking skin that was see-through. I could see its veins and organs, and its face was melted and smushed, but also inflated in all the wrong areas. Black scraggly hair fell across its round shoulders and two circles of black formed its eyes.

It was truly something from a nightmare.

"Get on my back," Arryn whispered so that only I could hear.

As soon as I jumped onto him, the figure melted down onto the ground into a liquid and flowed towards us. It grew back up and wrapped around Arryn's legs, gluing him to the ground.

"Arryn!" I screamed as the blob-like creature seemed to swallow Arryn into the ground. We were sinking deeper and deeper. The clumpy liquid now reached my ankle.

We were sinking into the ground, fast.

Arryn was frantically looking around before his vines slid up around my thighs, forming a seat of some sort, and then stretched around his shoulders and back to the top of his back to form wings. They flapped as hard as they could, but it only pulled us out a few inches.

The blob was sinking us into the ground faster than his wings could fly us out.

"Amara, my wings aren't working!"

Scrambling for an idea I felt a small box in my pocket and remembered the candle I had lit earlier back at the castle. I must have put the matches into my pocket.

I jumped off Arryn's back into the blob creature, the liquid now up to my neck.

"Amara! NO. What are you doing?" Arryn screamed.

"Just trust me!" I said holding my hands above my head as I struck the match against the rough piece of sandpaper that was glued to the side of the small metal box.

Come on.

I struck the box over and over, swiping the match across it.

It wouldn't light.

The liquid was now covering my mouth and nose. I couldn't breathe. I looked over to Arryn and all I could see was the tips of his silver hair.

This was it.

It was now or never.

We were going to die.

I held my arms above the blob, only my hands were visible by that point. I tried over and over to light the match.

Just then, I saw the flare of light and threw the small match onto the blob of liquid.

There were no flames, no fire, the creature simply cried out in pain as the blob dissipated and evaporated into thin air.

Arryn gasped and then began to throw up a clear thick liquid.

I rushed over to rub his back as he was panting.

We both stilled as we observed the clear liquid that he just threw up form together and inch away like a small snail.

We grimaced as we looked at each other.

"How did you know that would work?" he questioned as he still struggled to catch his breath.

"I didn't," I shook my head. "I just had to do *something*."

He nodded and then got to his feet. "Let's get the hell out of here."

27

Arryn ran through the woods so fast it felt like we were traveling at the speed of light. I begged him to slow down so that he didn't deplete his magic, but he refused. He said he would rather pass out from exhaustion than see me tricked by the forest again or come across another one of those... *creatures*. We were going so fast that the woods didn't even have a chance to manipulate our minds.

We came up upon the edge of the forest, it dropped down into a large cove surrounded by craggy rocks with steaming water in the middle that connected to a river. The fog lifted from it and moved in the way you would expect a whisper to look as if it could take a physical form. The cove resembled a giant cauldron with a mysterious liquid bubbling inside.

As the fog lifted, there was a plot of land in the middle. Tall skeleton looking bushes with branches curling around themselves wrapped around the outer edge of the land. The branches had sharp thorns sticking out from every direction, probably to keep out any visitors that dared to enter.

However, something told me the witches didn't get many visitors.

"Let's go," Arryn whispered as he slowly climbed down the rocks. He reached his hand out to help me down.

As he was helping me to balance, I somehow *still* managed to slip on some wet moss covering one of the jagged rocks. I fell back with a yelp before arms wrapped around my back steadying me. I dropped down into Arryn's chest and his beautiful golden eyes peered down at me.

"Thank you." I couldn't say it enough times for how often he was saving me. Not just from danger, but from a life that I didn't want.

I didn't know it at the time, but when Arryn framed me and got me banished, he was really saving me from a life that I knew deep down wasn't my fate. Because he was *my fate*. "For saving me… and my heart," I breathed. "For being the light that guided me out of my ever-so-dark world."

I didn't know if it was the fear that the forest instilled in me and how I realized how quickly I could die, but I wanted to get it all out right then. I needed him to know how I felt in case I never got another chance.

A light smile appeared on his face. One that always lit up my world, no matter how bleak it seemed. A smile that was equivalent to the sun rising, lighting up the darkest of nights.

"I am glad that I could be the one to save you… and *your heart*. All these years, in a kingdom of light, you are the brightest thing in my life." His eyes dropped to my lips and he placed his palm over my heart. "I—"

He threw us backward, his hand behind the back of my head as we crashed into the rocks. He took most of the impact from the fall, but my body still reverberated with pain.

"Amara, *RUN!*" Arryn screamed as he pulled me off the rocks. Before I could even take a step, something sharp and stiff wrapped around my ankle and yanked causing me to fall again. This time, Arryn's hand wasn't there to protect my head as it banged against a rock. The world spun and a ring reverberated through my ear drums.

Dizziness took over my vision, but not enough to prevent me from seeing a branch of thorns wrap around both of Arryn's ankles and drag him down. He slid against the rocks, against the ground, and through the water until he was sucked beyond the wall of thorns.

My back screamed in protest along with my ankle as I got to my feet. I frantically looked around trying to think of a plan. Anything that could save him.

Follow, that voice in my head seemed to whisper.

So I did.

❀ ❀ ❀

I sprinted through the water, not caring that it was up to my knees and that the water was ice cold.

Or that my knees were buckling and my whole body was buckling in pain from the fall.

I went right up to the mess of branches and thorns that formed the wall. As I got closer, I could see the thorns… *moving*. It was as if they were alive or spelled to be a living gate of some sort.

"May I—come in?" I choked out. I figured that if they were alive enough to capture Arryn, then maybe they could understand words.

Nothing happened, and they still blocked the way in.

The branches swirled and curled around each other like a pit full of snakes.

Snakes with *thorns*.

I took a step forward hoping they would move aside. I had a small knife, but I doubted that it would do anything against them. It would probably just anger them even more.

As I crept forward, I noticed that the thorns were moving to the side, as if they were *letting* me in.

These branches made of a different type of magic seemed to bend down for me as I limped past. My blood buzzed as I passed by them as if there were a connection or some sort of tether between us.

I continued on, walking slowly so I wouldn't spook the thorns.

They uncurled to a point where I could see a cottage surrounded by trees.

I decided to walk the perimeter to search for Arryn and to hopefully avoid any witches.

I slowly trudged along the wall of thorns, being careful not to step on one or get too close to them.

It was then I heard breathing.

Inhale.

Exhale.

It was soft, faint. As if whatever, *whoever* it was, was struggling to breathe. My head turned up to the branches above me, and suddenly I couldn't breathe at the sight of *who* was wrapped in branches of thorns, pinned up with arms and legs outstretched. His eyes were closed and his silver hair dangled down past his forehead.

Arryn.

My heart completely stopped, and it was an effort to breathe.

Think, Amara. Think.

There was only one way to get him down. One way for me to reach him.

I pulled the golden ribbon that was tied around my top and used it to secure my hair back. Hooking one foot up onto a branch below me and wrapping my hands around the branches above me, I hoisted myself up.

I winced at the pain in my ankle but continued to carefully climb up the wall, making sure to not grab any thorns or step on them either. It was tedious to avoid every single thorn, but they were as large as knives and I did *not* want to get poked by one.

As I neared the top where Arryn was, I looked down. My stomach turned at how high from the ground I was. It didn't look this high standing below, but from the top, it seemed as high as Arryn's castle.

I turned my head and closed my eyes as I inhaled sharply.

I can do this.

I climbed up the last few feet. "Arryn? Arryn?" I said several times.

His eyes were closed and his face was in a calm state as if he was asleep. He wouldn't respond, and I checked him for injuries, but there was nothing. He had already healed from being smacked and dragged around on the rocks by the branches.

Another perk of being a fate. At that moment, I was glad that he wasn't human. He probably would have died being dragged along the rocks that way if he was like me.

It was as if he was in a very deep sleep. Like some sort of spell had been put on him.

I began to carefully pluck the thorns from around his wrist. They were stiff and had a strong hold on him, but with a little force, I was able to pull them off from one of his wrists. When I reached for the other one, I felt a prick in my shoulder.

My head snapped to see that the tip of a thorn had punctured my shoulder when I reached to free his other wrist. Blood dripped from it and fell to the ground below.

My grip on the branches started to loosen as my vision became blurry. Before I knew it, I was falling backward toward the ground.

"Well, well, well. What do we have here?" I heard a smooth woman's voice call out just as my back cracked when it met the ground and I fell out of consciousness.

28

I awoke to the smell of amber and myrrh. There were candles lit all around me, so many that for a second I thought I was back in the underground. The only reason I realized I wasn't, was because of the skylight window on the ceiling. The night sky and the moonlight shone brightly through it.

I sat up to find a woman sitting across from me, just staring. Her hair was a deep burgundy color so dark it almost looked black. Where the moonlight touched her hair, it glowed white and shimmered like stars.

Her cheekbones were so high that small indents were made in the middle of her cheeks. Eyes of emerald green stared into me, examined me.

I looked around and realized we were in a witch's home. There were spices everywhere, and various plants and different types of sage. Candles of all colors were placed on every flat surface with silver stands holding them up. Bookshelves lined each wall with spell books scattered and placed along each shelf.

I heard a rustling next to me, and when I saw Arryn sit up, my body immediately calmed.

He's alive. He's okay.

"My apologies, Arryn. If I knew you were coming I would have called off the thorns." The woman who seemed to be only a few years older than me said in a smug tone.

I looked at Arryn and then at the witch.

"How do you know his name?" I said nervously.

"Oh, so she speaks," she purred. Her eyes moved quickly from Arryn to me, and I could see the thoughts swirling in her mind. "Well, he is the king of the Light Kingdom, isn't he?"

Beside me, I could hear Arryn let out a breath of relief.

"I am Selene Darkhart. The most powerful witch in this cove." She threw her hand up and uncurled it outward. "Some may even call me the queen of the witches."

She threw a smug grin towards Arryn. "Now… why have you come?" Her voice lowered and all expression fell from her face.

"We—" Arryn cleared his throat. "We have come because my brother, Keiran, has put magic on her, a spell of some sort." Arryn gestured to me.

"Hmmm…" She tapped her long bony fingers on the side of her chair. "What's in it for me?" Those pits of emerald darted to Arryn.

He clicked his tongue in frustration and then sighed. "Ten minutes."

"An hour," she bit back.

"Fine," he said, offering up his arm to the witch.

She grinned as she began to cut over an old scar in the middle of Arryn's hand.

I filed that information away to ask him about it later.

Confusion must have been etched onto my face as she started to explain. "An hour of his life in exchange for my help." My face dropped as I beheld the drops of blood that she squeezed from his hand into a glass jar. "Relax, since he's immortal it doesn't do anything to him. An hour of his life is like taking one strand of hair from your head. You won't even know it's missing… The only consequence is that he will have to live with himself for helping a witch," she mocked.

"Why do you need an hour of his life? What are you going to use it for?" I asked.

Her face turned grim, "You never know when you're going to need more time."

Arryn glared at her as he ripped back his hand and wrapped a scrap of cloth around it.

"Enough. You've got your *time*, now tell us how to break Amara's hex," he snapped.

"Oh right…" she said as she added some ingredients to the blood, whispered a chant, and then swallowed it. "About that… No one *put* a curse or a spell on her."

My shoulders dropped, but Arryn only became more tense.

"What do you mean?" he growled.

"*She. Is. Not. Cursed.* I sensed no magic put on her, and my magic would call to anything ancient…" The witch cocked her head as she examined me head to toe, confusion on her face. "No curse was put on her… Where is she from—?"

She was interrupted as Arryn's vines took form and began to grow out from his wrists and around her faster than she could finish her sentence. They squeezed around her waist, binding her arms to her sides.

"You tricked me," he said, pulling his vines around her tighter.

"*You* asked a question. *I* answered it," she growled right back. "There was no spell cast on her. All of it was *her* choice." Her words seared through me like I had laid down on hot coals.

If it wasn't a spell…

"It wasn't me. Something was drawing me in, something I couldn't control," I countered. "I would know what thoughts are mine and which aren't. There was something… *else.*"

The witch laughed. "Yes, there is much you can't control."

Much I can't control?

"We are done here." Arryn yanked his vines back and they snapped back into his wrist, taking on the form of markings once more.

"I'll throw these into our bargain. Free of charge." She tossed Arryn a few vials of a purple liquid.

"What is it?" He snarled as he caught them.

"A tonic to prevent the tricks of the woods from infiltrating your mind. It also protects you against the pricks of the thorns. This tonic makes you immune to ancient magic."

Arryn peered into the vials. "How do I know I can trust that's what's really in these?"

Selene stalked forward and seductively took one of the bottles from Arryn and swigged down half the bottle. "I would never poison a *king*." Her mouth dropped open on the last word before she glared at me and sneered.

I sensed some tension between her and Arryn. Tension mostly coming from Arryn's side and... something else from Selene. Whatever that *something* was, it twisted my stomach into knots.

"Thank you," I cut in. "For the tonics."

I wanted to rip her beautiful, long hair out for talking that way to Arryn, but I chose to be polite. Especially since she already didn't like me *and* because she was a witch.

She nodded once as she crossed her arms.

As Arryn and I turned to leave, she grabbed my arm and pulled me in close as she whispered, "If you ever wish to seek the truth, you know where to find me."

When she pulled away, I felt that ancient magic brush up against my skin from where she held me. It felt the same way as the thorns did. Like there was some tether between us, something that linked us.

I ripped my arm back and followed after Arryn.

I had so many questions racing through my head, but the first thing we needed to do was get out of there.

❁ ❁ ❁

It turned out Selene *had* been telling the truth after all. After we took the tonic, we were able to safely pass through the woods without any delusions or tricks. She had given us an extra vial, so Arryn stored it away in his office.

At dinner, things were a bit awkward. There were words unspoken between Arryn and I that he had almost said back at the cove. I had wanted to hear him say it in the moment. It was all I wanted to hear. Now, it was like I was waiting for something to happen that should've already happened, but didn't. It made us both act on edge. Mostly because we both knew what he was about to say on those rocks.

Everything happens according to fate though. It wasn't the right moment for it if fate had intervened.

Throughout dinner, Selene's words echoed through my mind.

"If you ever wish to seek the truth, you know where to find me."

She had said those words to me as if she knew more about myself than I did.

The truth.

Part of me felt like it was some sort of mind game, a way to drive me crazy, but the other half of me was curious. I was *always* curious. Someday, it would get me into trouble, and I knew that, but I couldn't help it.

"I am glad you guys made it back safely. I was starting to worry when you still weren't back after a few hours," Caris admitted as she dove into her food.

As much as I wanted to smile and pretend to be in a cheerful mood, I couldn't ignore the thoughts that plagued my brain and the desire to know more.

I also couldn't stop thinking about the weird tension between Selene and Arryn. I wanted to ask him about it on the way back to the castle, but I didn't know *what* to even ask.

"Actually, I am not feeling very well," I said, pressing the back of my palm to my forehead and gripping my stomach with my other hand. "I think I am going to head to bed." I stood up from my chair.

"Are you alright? I can come help you—" Arryn started to stand with me.

"No! I think I just need to rest… I will see you tomorrow. Hopefully, I will feel better by then." I spoke as if everything was normal.

"As you wish." Hurt seemed to flash through those golden eyes, but it was replaced with compassion in an instant. "I hope you feel better."

I flashed him a smile and then headed towards my bedroom and opened the door, closing it a second later. On quiet toes, I stepped away from my door and towards Arryn's office.

I opened a few drawers, pushing around papers and books before I found what I was looking for in the bottom drawer of the desk.

I grabbed the extra tonic and then headed for the balcony in my bedroom.

29

This is crazy. I thought as I peered over my balcony. The white wall of the castle beneath with ivy vines wrapped around it. If they were strong enough, I could climb down quietly without anyone realizing it.

I felt horrible for lying to Arryn, but I knew that he would say it was too dangerous or insist on going back *with* me.

This was something I had to do for myself. I wasn't even sure why because the witch could have just been lying to me.

Either way, she acted like she knew something that I didn't, and I had to find out what it was.

I reached my leg down over the balcony and then stepped onto the vine. I tested it by slowly shifting my full weight onto it.

The vines seemed sturdy enough, so I let go of the balcony and then began my descent, refusing to look down the entire time or I would've climbed back up.

I jumped off the wall when I reached the bottom.

Breaking into the stables, I stole a horse that I knew was one of the faster ones. I had noticed her when we took the carriage into town that day. She stood out from the other horses as she huffed anytime we took a break.

She was so tall that I struggled to mount her. The dark coat was as black as night, and she huffed a breath into the cool night air as I sat up onto her back.

I spun in a circle to remember what direction Arryn had taken us in. I knew North was the Kingdom of Darkness, so that meant… I turned to the left to face the west.

West was the way to Witches Cove.

I tapped my heel into the horse's backside and she took off into a trot.

The voice appeared for all but a few seconds to warn me with one single word.

Mistake.

I pushed that inner voice out and continued on, ignoring it. My curiosity convinced me that my gut feeling was once again just *wrong*.

After miles of riding, I finally reached the entrance to the forest.

I swigged down the tonic that would prevent my mind from succumbing to the tricks of the woods.

When I reached the edge of the forest where it dropped down into rocks, I tied up the horse to a tree and gave her a gentle pat on the back before climbing down, carefully this time as I was now on my own.

The entire climb down I wrestled with myself about why I even came back here. How it was a mistake, and that she was most likely messing with me, but I just couldn't shake the thought that there was something I needed to find out.

I could have sworn something tugged on my mind at that thought.

Climbing down the jagged rocks was much harder without Arryn there to keep me steady. Though I didn't *need* him to help me, it was a lot easier and less life threatening. I knew that if I slipped he would be there in an instant to catch me.

As terrifying as it was, I slowly made my way down the rocks and splashed through the shallow water.

When I reached that wall of thorns, they all bent back again to form a path for me. I carefully treaded through them, and they closed back up behind me as soon as I passed through.

I made my way to the cottage, and before I could even knock on the door, it swung open to reveal Selene standing with her arms crossed.

"I knew you would be back." She stepped sideways and gestured for me to enter.

I knew deep down that it was a bad idea, but I stepped in anyway. It seemed like in that single decision alone I had sealed my fate. For better or worse I didn't know.

"Sit," she ordered and the door slammed shut on a phantom wind.

I gulped and then took a seat at the kitchen table. She sat across from me and began to light bundles of a plant that smelled earthy and slightly sweet. She began wafting it around in the air before setting it in a dish in between us.

"It protects our conversation, from those who could be listening," she clarified.

I turned around to glance around the cottage. "Protect us from who? Nobody is here."

She smiled and blinked at me as if I had just said the dumbest thing she had ever heard. "Not people here, I said people who could be *listening*. There are those who do not have to be physically present somewhere to listen in on a conversation… Plus, the dead are *always* listening."

I kept my face stoic even though a cold chill went up my spine and the hair on my arms stood up straight.

"You said that if I wished to seek the truth to find you again... here I am," I said. "What is the *'truth'* that you speak of?"

Selene snickered as she sat back in her chair with one arm relaxed up onto the side. "You do not feel the call? The ancient fate magic, it doesn't call to you?"

My stomach dropped as I recalled the strange pull that I felt from the thorns and then from Selene. Arryn had mentioned that the witches used a different type of magic... ancient magic.

"Raw magic, the magic that fates were born with- Spells, curses, and hexes, those are different. A different type of ancient magic that is drawn from something else. It is not so simple as light and dark."

Was she saying that I somehow... had some sort of connection to it?

I remained silent. I wasn't going to tell her anything. I wasn't sure if she would use it against me or not.

"Very well. Do not tell me. I already know the answer anyway." She tilted her head.

"What would it mean— if I did *feel the call*?" I asked.

"That... is for you to figure out on your own. All I can tell you is that darkness calls to darkness. I can sense, feel, and use magic, but I am not a fate teller," she snapped. Something told me she knew more than what she was letting on.

"I risked a lot to come back here, and now you won't even tell me what you promised? You knew enough to tell me that there was some sort of *truth* that I wasn't aware of. Unless that was another one of your tricks." My mind started putting pieces together that I should've realized before.

"I promised nothing," Selene scoffed. "You risked a lot? How so? Does Arryn not know that you're here?" she inquired.

That gut feeling told me to lie.

"No, he knows. He is here with me, but I told him that I wanted to speak with you alone," I lied.

"Hmm... very well then. Be on your way, I have nothing more to tell you other than to listen to that call. Let it guide you rather than trying to guide it."

"Thank you for your time," I said nervously making my way to the door.

"Oh, and one more thing," Selene purred and I paused in the doorway. I turned around to see her with her hands behind her back.

"You're a horrible liar." She smirked as she pulled out a small branch with a thorn on it, and faster than I could run away, she stabbed it into my arm, right where that bite mark from Keiran had been.

Words failed me, and my vision started to fail too. I dropped to the ground and all I saw was Selene's black boots clicking toward me as I fell into a deep sleep.

30

My eyes cracked open slowly as I felt the springy mattress beneath me and beheld the dark stone in front of my eyes. Candles lit up my room in a warm glow that made the roses seem as if there were halos of light behind them.

   I pulled back the beige comforter and stepped out of bed. When I reached the kitchen, my mother and father had been sitting at the table eating breakfast in silence.

   "Good morning," I mumbled as I took my usual seat.

   My mother filled my plate, but only half as much as she put onto my father's.

The white gruel was especially boring that morning. I wasn't sure why since it was all I knew, but for some reason that morning it tasted *worse*.

No one spoke during the meal, but it was nothing out of the ordinary.

After breakfast, I tied back my locks, making sure to slick down all stray hairs. I then slipped on the usual linen dress that I always wore.

Trudging down the dark hallways, I felt my shoes scrape against the rough stone floors as if it were an effort to move. I didn't feel tired, but it felt like I was trying to run in water. Every step demanded a conscious struggle.

When I finally made my way to the gathering hall, I tried to ignore the weight in my chest. It felt like when you forget something that was on the tip of your tongue but can't remember what it was for the life of you.

The whole morning felt strange.

I ignored my gut feeling that something was *wrong*.

Prancing through the cafeteria, I saw Poppy sitting at one of the tables with Sam.

"Hi!" I said as I plopped down next to her. I felt as if I hadn't spoken to her in ages.

She didn't speak, or even acknowledge my presence.

Had I done something to upset her? Even if I did though, it was unlike Poppy to not say what was on her mind.

"Did I do something?" I asked her quietly so that no one else could hear.

She continued to ignore me, laughing at some joke that Sam made.

That was another thing that was off. Sam made a joke, since when did he not act shy? Especially around other people.

Poppy continued talking with Sam, pretending that I was invisible.

I must have done something truly awful to make her act this way towards me.

I turned around, scanning the gathering hall before stopping to see where Mason sat. He wasn't in his usual spot, but there was someone… someone with black velvet hair, and eyes so dark they could be described as midnight back. He was sitting where Mason usually had. His eyes were scanning around the gathering spot, starting from the far left until—

His eyes stopped on me.

If looks could kill, I would be dead. He stood and marched towards me, ignoring everyone in his sight, walking *through* them.

What is going on?

"Wake up," he snarled as he stalked toward me.

"What are you talking about?" I asked, my voice coming out echoed and muffled as if my head was underwater. "I am awake-"

"Wake *up*."

"Who are you?"

His angry expression turned into something like amusement as he spoke the one word that pulled me out of where I had been.

"*Keiran.*"

❀ ❀ ❀

My eyes flung open with a large gasp. My only view was of the night sky above, and it was… moving.

It took me all but a few seconds to realize I was lying in the back of a carriage. I looked around at my surroundings as we passed through the woods. Tall skeletal trees seemed to sway and curve with the howl of the wind. It was completely dark, the only light was the beams of moonlight that shone through the bare trees.

I turned around and peeked over the edge of the carriage to see who was steering the horses.

Selene.

It all came back to me then. Memories of Arryn, Caris, Keiran, and Selene…

I must have been under some sort of sleeping spell, the same one that had been put on Arryn when we arrived the first time. I then remembered Selene had lunged a thorn into my skin before I fell asleep, believing I was back underground.

Selene was the only one to lift the spell on Arryn, so how did I wake up?

"*Wake up,*" Keiran's voice from my dream replayed in my head.

I ignored the fact that it had been his voice to take me out of my slumber and began thinking of how I was going to get out of this mess.

To my surprise, my ankles and hands hadn't been tied, and nothing was keeping me to the carriage. Selene must have had so much trust in her spell that she didn't even think to tie me up.

What could she have possibly been getting out of this? Who wanted me that badly that they would make a deal with a witch to—

Oh no.

I realized there was only one person who I knew would do that.

Suddenly the carriage came to a halt and I heard Selene jump off, her boots crunching in the autumn leaves as she stepped away from the carriage. I stayed lying down, pretending that I was still asleep in case she walked over.

"Do you have what you promised?" a male voice that, to my surprise, wasn't Keiran's said. The man's voice was gruff and hoarse. He sounded older and cold. It was familiar to me, but I wasn't sure where I had heard that voice before.

"Yes. Do *you* have what was promised to me?" Selene purred.

My curiosity once again got the best of me as I peeked over the side of the carriage, just enough to see two silhouettes talking. The one that was obviously too tall and large to be Selene, handed her a bag.

From what I could see, it seemed to be a bundle of flowers with large thorns sticking out from the sides. The petals were dark purple and iridescent. A silver glow bounced through the purpled-hued petals as if they were translucent, and the thorns on the sides were also glass-like, but deadly-looking.

What is her obsession with thorns?

"Just the thorns. The rest of the flower doesn't do anything." He crossed his arms and looked toward the carriage. I ducked and tried to steady my breathing, hoping that he hadn't seen me. I had to get out of there. "Do you have her?" My whole body froze as a shudder went from my neck down my spine.

"Yes. She's in the back… sleeping," she said, uninterested.

"And will she… *stay* asleep?" The male asked.

Selene scoffed. "Yes, she's under a spell that will keep her sleeping until I say for her to wake up… I still don't see why she can't be killed here. I need to make sure that she dies before—"

My heart was now in my throat as it pounded like it was about to burst.

Before what?

"She will, but not here. Orders from— I don't need to explain myself to you, *witch*." He growled the last word like there was no greater insult.

I knew what Selene looked like without even having to see her face.

"Take her then," she spat.

Think Amara, think.

I looked around the empty carriage trying to find a way out of this. Fear whirled around inside me, creating a cloud of darkness that grew with each passing second.

"Give in, Amara." That voice appeared.

I was out of options. I didn't know what else to do, so I did. I let it consume me, take over me, my soul, my *body*. I felt lighter as I tucked myself into a dark corner of the carriage, letting my body morph and blend into the darkness.

The man peered over the edge of the carriage.

My blood stilled, and my breathing stopped as he looked around, and then his eyes stopped on me. Looking right at me, *through me*.

I looked down at my hands and turned them around as they seemed to blend into the shadows of the carriage. Sweat began to bead on my forehead as I gulped in confusion.

"There is no one here," he snarled. "If this is some sort of trap you will be sorry—"

"What the *hell* are you going on about?" Selene snapped back as she marched over to take a look for herself. "No... How did she—? She must have broken the spell somehow— I—" she stuttered. "We need to look for her. Go. NOW!" she screamed at the man.

As he turned to look for me, she took out a thorn and stabbed him in the gut with it. He immediately passed out into a deep sleep.

I took this as my cue to run, to get as far away as possible from whatever the hell was happening here.

My body seemed to float in the darkness as I crawled over the top of the carriage, taking back my physical form as my feet touched the ground. I looked under the carriage to see if Selene was still there, but she was gone.

I didn't waste one moment before I started running in the opposite direction of where the carriage had been heading. I didn't care how fast my heart was beating or how labored my breaths were. I was numb to it all as I ran through the dark forest.

I turned back to see if I was being followed, and when I saw that no one was there I faced back around and slammed into what felt like a metal wall. Only there was nothing there. It was as if there was some invisible wall that formed to keep me from leaving the forest. It was then that I felt a hand rip back my hair and pull me down to the ground. I screamed out in pain as Selene stood over me, her face twisted into something much more deadly than it had been before.

"*How. Did. You. Break. My. Spell!*" she ground out. "Answer me!" She yanked back on my hair again.

"I don't know!" I screamed back. "I didn't even know I was under a spell. I had been dreaming, and then Keiran appeared—"

She paused and then dropped my hair as she took several steps back from me. "Keiran? *Keiran* entered your dreams? How is that possible-" Fear seemed to wash over her face and turn her skin pale. I enjoyed seeing her frightened, but to know it was because of Keiran… it made me uncomfortable to know how dangerous he was and how close he had been to me.

She stopped talking and then pulled out a small knife. "This needs to end. Now," she growled and ran towards me with the knife angled upward.

"No, please. Selene, please!" I begged. Even though it was pitch black outside, my vision was able to see shadows and silhouettes after years of being underground. My eyes had adjusted and gotten used to the world being dark. The darkness, I realized, was not my enemy. It was my friend. Different from the darkness of the dark fates, this darkness. True darkness in its most pure form, the absence of light… it was *my* playground.

I decided that in that moment I wouldn't be saved. Not by Arryn, Caris, or even Keiran. I would be saved by Amara.

I took a deep breath as I lunged forward and rolled into a pile of leaves, and Selene plunged her knife into the tree that had been behind me. She stood there grunting trying to pull the knife out from the thick bark, but she wasn't quick enough. I saw the secret pocket that she kept the thorns in. It was a belt that hung around her waist. It seemed like a regular belt, or an accessory to the black flowing dress that she was wearing, but it was secretly a pouch for her to keep her spelled thorns.

I snatched one from her pocket, and before she could realize what I was doing, I drove it into her back, pushing it hard enough for it to be painful. The same way she had done it to me.

"NO!" she growled before falling to the ground in a sleep so sound she almost looked kind, peaceful even.

I blew out the breath I had been holding in and then sunk to my knees. Shaking, I dropped my arms and my head down in relief.

"Amara?" I heard a faint voice call out from the direction I had been running. I heard the light in his voice, the goodness that wrapped around me and always comforted my fears.

"Arryn!" I shouted back.

He was there in an instant.

"Amara," he let out a relieved breath as he took me in his arms and kissed the top of my head. "Why did you leave? Why wouldn't you tell me? What happened?" He pulled back for only a moment so that he could survey my body for any injuries.

"I'm sorry," was all I could manage to say. I would explain everything later, but right then all I needed was to feel him and forget everything that had just happened. My eyes began to burn as he pulled me back into his embrace, realizing how sorry I truly was.

Every mistake and misstep that I had made that night seemed to dissipate with the warmth of his touch.

"We can talk about it later. Let's just get you home," he whispered into my ear as he stroked the back of my head soothing every nerve in my body.

❦ ❦ ❦

"What did the witch tell you, exactly?" Arryn looked up as he took a sip from his drink. I was wrapped in a blanket beside the fire as I told him everything that happened, down to when I stabbed Selene with her own spelled thorns.

"Not much. I was stupid for thinking that she knew anything, it had all been a trick to get me there. What she said didn't even make sense."

"What did she say?" he asked again.

It seemed strange how interested he was in what the witch told me. He had never been so… *pushy* before— about anything.

"Nothing really, just something about ancient magic," I clarified. "And that 'darkness calls to darkness,' whatever that means."

"What about ancient magic?" He asked quickly.

"Arryn, I don't remember. Why do you need to know so badly?" I questioned him.

His expression changed from concerned to cheerful in just a few seconds, "I don't need to know, I just wanted to know what lies she spewed into your head. You can't trust a witch. It was a bad idea to ever go there in the first place."

He nervously brushed aside his hair before bringing his index finger and thumb to his chin. His eyes darted back and forth as if he couldn't calm his thoughts.

A look I knew all too well.

My gut feeling told me there was more to it than that, but I chose to believe his words.

31

It had been a few days since Selene tried to sell me off and then kill me. I wasn't sure what Arryn did with her comatose body, and I didn't really care either. Part of me felt bad at the fact that he could've dumped her in a lake and I wouldn't have batted an eye. Even though she tried to *kill* me, I didn't want her dead.

He said that he took her somewhere that she would be safe, but not where she could be found. That was enough for me.

Even though everything was now fine, good even, there was still a pit in my stomach. Keiran had been too quiet. He hadn't made any more attempts to get me to go with him, but I knew that he would strike again at some point. I just didn't know when.

"Hi, Amara," Caris said softly as she entered the library. "I just wanted to check and see how you were doing… after *everything*."

"You mean after Selene tried to kill me? I'm great," I said sarcastically. She flinched as if I had just punched her in the stomach and then guilt immediately gripped onto me. "I'm sorry, I didn't mean to be rude. I'm just a little on edge."

"Understandably so." She attempted to smile but her eyes didn't follow suit for once.

"Why did she try to kill me? I don't understand. She brought me to trade with that man and then… she killed him. Well, put him under the sleep spell. I just don't get it. And why would she give me away for some flowers in exchange? None of it makes sense." I closed my eyes and exhaled sharply. "There's something I don't know, and I don't like not knowing things, Caris. I don't like feeling powerless and unaware… if there's something that you guys aren't telling me…"

For a second it seemed like she was about to throw up, but then her expression turned cold. It was strange to see her with an expression so opposite from what she usually bore.

"No. There is nothing. We know as much as you," she said flatly. "Just… trust Arryn and everything will be okay." Her tone sounded as if she was trying to convince herself more than me. "What you two have is very special, focus on that." As she made to leave the room, I realized that she was right.

I had been so focused on the things that I didn't know instead of what I did- What was right in front of me. Arryn and I... we had something beautiful, *rare*. I wasn't going to ruin that based on my stupid gut feelings or because of my curiosity.

I decided that it was time to take things into my own hands too, instead of waiting for them to happen. I wrote Arryn a note and left it on his desk and then got to work.

❀ ❀ ❀

Caris said that she would be gone for the day and into the night, so it worked out perfectly. Arryn was out in the town speaking to his subjects, and he wouldn't be back until later. It gave me just enough time to set up.

I ran around the castle like a mad woman, stealing all the tall candles in metal stands that they owned. I set them up in my bedroom on every flat surface.

I then picked several roses from the garden and plucked off all the petals, scattering them on the floor from the entryway up the stairs to lead into his office first and then into my bedroom.

It wasn't the most impressive thing ever, but it was a romantic gesture, one that I knew he would appreciate even though it could've been more.

I lit every single candle in my room and then plopped down onto my bed laying on my back. I thought I might rest while I waited for Arryn to get home.

A deep breath surged from me as I brought my hands to my chest and clasped them over my heart. It was beating quickly at the thought of him. I smiled and turned my head to the side as if I was trying to hide from myself. I never knew what it felt like to be infatuated with someone. In all those years underground, I had never felt this way about anybody. We were taught to marry and breed, that was it. But here, I felt like a part of me was unlocking. Feelings and sensations had emerged that I never knew were possible.

It felt as if the first twenty years of my life were a blurry mess, and I finally could see clearly.

My door suddenly swung open and I lifted my head just enough to see Arryn standing in the doorway. A soft smile took over his lips.

"I assume this is all for me?" He looked around as he took in the candles and rose petals scattered over the bed.

"It is…" I sat up. "Unless there is some other fate named Arryn who is king of the Light Kingdom? If so feel free to send him in."

Did I just say that?

His brows rose and he shut the door behind him. He waved the note that I left in his office as he spoke, "I believe there's only one." He made his way towards my bed. He leaned over me and brought his lips to meet mine. The glow that shined out from him coated our lips in warmth from the sun.

"The note said there was a surprise waiting in here for me…"

I slowly lifted the covers back to reveal the golden nightgown that left nothing to the imagination. His eyes went wide as he took in every inch of my form.

"*This*… is the best surprise I have ever received," he said as his stare lingered on the thin fabric.

"And that's not all of it," I murmured as I stood and took his face in my hands, holding the sides of his strong jaw.

His eyes darted between both of mine back and forth until they settled on my lips.

"Arryn, the past months with you I have learned so much about the world. About *living*. I didn't know what life could be outside of the darkness underground, but you showed me a life that I never dreamed I could even have. You showed me how to love."

I placed a hand over his chest and felt his pulse beating just as quickly as mine. "I never knew true love, and now that I met you I know what it is."

"Amara," he whispered and his breath mingled with mine.

"I love you," I finally said, pushing through all the anxiety of whether he would say it back or not.

All my fears disappeared as he smiled so wide I thought his cheeks would tear open.

"I love you too. I have never loved anything or anyone as much as I love you."

"Then show me," I purred.

His expression twisted into pure delight as he went in to kiss me while he reached for the bottom of my dress, rolling it up and scrunching it beneath his hand. He yanked me forward with his other arm to bring me to my feet.

"You really love me?" he asked.

"Yes." I had never been more sure of anything in my life.

He lunged forward and took me in his arms.

His hands were placed around my backside and lifted me up. Then his lips met mine, and he kissed me. It was more passionate than any of the other ones. *Deeper.*

He pulled back and examined me with confusion etched into his forehead.

"What?" I asked.

Before he could answer a loud boom of thunder sounded from outside.

The window inside my room that led to the balcony cracked and shattered. Pieces flew to the floor as a black cloud drifted inside.

"Get back!" Arryn ordered.

I backed up towards the far wall of my bedroom as I watched the cloud enter through the broken window. Arryn was there in a second, his arm out in front of me as a shield.

The cloud's mist swirled and then took a human-like shape. The mist faded and a tall man was left standing in its place.

Keiran.

32

Keiran's black eyes glowed with what seemed to be sparkles of darkness as he scanned my body.

I had to still my heart and keep my breathing steady.

Fight it, Amara! I screamed at myself as I seemed to slip back into that strange trance.

This time, it had been much weaker. I was able to push it aside and ignore it, just as I always ignored that voice in my head.

"Well, I do apologize for the poor timing Arryn," he winked. "It's nothing personal."

"Leave, Keiran," Arryn growled.

Keiran clicked his tongue. "What a terrible way to greet your brother." He brought a hand to his chest and puckered his bottom lip.

"Please, just leave. Do not start a war over this," Arryn pleaded.

Keiran snickered. "You say that as if a war would be something to deter me."

"Please," Arryn begged. Something inside me broke at the sight of him so helpless. If I didn't hate Keiran before, I did now.

"Save it," Keiran waved his hand in the air dismissing Arryn's plea.

"Amara, run. NOW!" Arryn shouted, turning to me.

Before I could even process what he said, Keiran was in front of me, those depthless black eyes peering into my very soul.

"I wonder… did our golden boy Arryn tell you what he has been doing? Why he took such a liking to a human girl? So quickly too…" Keiran ran a finger through a strand of my hair and I shuddered at his cold touch.

"Shut your mouth, Keiran," Arryn growled.

"Tell me, did our little self-righteous light fate ever tell you the *real* reason he kept you?" He tilted my chin up to force my gaze to his. "Answer me," he growled.

"No, and I don't care," I spat.

Arryn sprinted towards Keiran, his hand up with his vines shooting out toward Keiran's feet. Without an ounce of effort, darkness shot out from Keiran and pinned his vines to the ground, and covered his mouth so he was unable to talk. Arryn was now pinned in place by the darkness.

"You would think that by now you realize you can not beat me," Keiran growled at his brother. He then whipped his head to me and stalked forward. I was up against the wall, wishing there was more space for me to back up. It felt too familiar to that day in the art shop when his body was pressed up against mine, pinning me to the wall.

"You don't know about the curse then?" He laughed as my face twisted into confusion. "How delightful, Arryn kept you in the dark about... *everything*."

He looked around and his eyes stopped on the rose petals laid out on the bed and then to the candles scattered around the room. He let out a mocking laugh as his eyebrows raised and his black eyes widened.

Arryn was squirming to be released, but the darkness only held him tighter.

"Let him go, I don't care what you have to say. Just let him go and leave us alone," I growled into his face.

"How about I tell you, and then you can decide," he placed his hands into his pockets and then began. "There is a curse on these lands…" Arryn's muffled screams interrupted Keiran before a wall of darkness appeared between Arryn and us.

"There, now I can speak without any interruptions. As I was saying, there is a curse on these lands. One that began with the wrongful death of a fate because he fell in love with a human."

My bones turned to ice as a faint memory flashed into my mind. One of my mother. She was smiling and laughing, something she never did, as she told me a fairy tale of a land far away. A land that had a curse set upon it. I tried to remember how the story ended, how the curse could be broken, but I couldn't remember her words. It was as if something inside me blocked out that part of the memory completely.

"The only way for the lands to be cured and for the curse to be lifted is for a fate and a human to fall into love and for it to be sealed by a true love kiss." He smirked as my blood stilled and the light inside of me, the absolute bliss and happiness I had just felt moments ago, faded away into nothingness. "Looks like Arryn, was using you all along. *Trying* to get you to fall in love with him to break the curse —"

My breaths became labored and a loud ring sounded through my head as I physically felt my heart shatter into a million pieces. My heart was filled with so much love for Arryn, he consumed every part of my heart, and now… I felt the love drain out from me, leaving an empty hole in its wake.

"The only thing is... Arryn had it wrong. They can't merely *"fall in love,"* they must be *fated* to each other and *then* fall in love... And, if you were fated for each other, you would have known by now." He smiled as he dropped the darkness that prevented Arryn from seeing us. "It's unheard of for a fate and a mortal to be a fated match, so fate was never really on your side from the start."

As the wall of shadows fell, so did the tears from my eyes. I met Arryn's gaze and the look in his eyes was pure regret. Once again, he had lied to me. This time after he promised there would be no more lies. I could accept the first one, I got over it. But this... he used me. He tricked me into loving him, I was simply a pawn in a larger game that I had no idea of. Anger burned and roiled through me, heating every inch of my skin.

Keiran finally dropped the darkness that held Arryn's mouth closed.

"Amara, please listen to me. At first, yes I was trying to get you to love me. I wanted to break the curse, desperately. It has plagued the lands for two hundred years and has prevented our people and humans from living in peace, together. It is the reason for the soul reapers, the witches, all of it. They draw their power from the curse which is why Selene tried to kill—"

"*I. Don't. Care,*" I growled as I interrupted his apology. It was too late, too late for all of it. He had so many chances to tell me, and if he had, I probably would have still fallen for him. That's what hurt the most about all of this.

If he just trusted me enough to tell me from the beginning…

"Amara, I love you," he cried. It was the first time I had ever seen him shed tears. My heart cracked even more, but no matter how hard it was to see him sob, I had to protect *my* heart. I couldn't move past this. Maybe one day I would forgive him.

But it wouldn't be today.

And because of my heartbreak, I quite possibly made one of the most foolish decisions of my entire life.

I was so tired of having my fate set for me. Of not knowing how my life would turn out. First, it was the underground and my parents.

I had no choice and no say in anything, and then Arryn…

I thought that he gave me freedom. Showed me what life could be like, but he had been manipulating me the entire time, knowing I would fall for him.

It was all fake.

It all started with a lie.

No more.

I would no longer be the result of other people's actions. I would take *my* life back, and choose how it would go.

My own parents hadn't loved me. I thought Arryn could fill that void, but it was silly of me to think so.

I am unlovable.

And in that moment it was clear.

I thought that he was it for me. That Arryn was everything that I had been missing, but he showed me that true love doesn't exist… Because if what we had was all a lie, then it can't exist at all.

As my mind spiraled, I felt the darkness wrap around my heart and strangle it until I felt no more. It was as if every nerve in my body went numb. A grey hue formed over the world, but the pain stopped.

I felt nothing.

Cared for nothing.

I turned to Keiran, meeting my eyes with his. Those pools of darkness seemed to glimmer just before I said two words that would forever change the course of my life.

"Take me," I breathed as I wiped a single tear from my cheek.

He wasn't worth my tears.

Keiran's mouth curled upward into a smile so devious it sent a cold chill through my entire body.

"Amara, NO!" Arryn screamed, still bound at the ankles by Keiran's darkness.

"I give you permission to take me," I repeated without a glance at Arryn.

Keiran grabbed my hand, too fast for me to change my mind, and then we were a cloud of dark mist, floating through the sky.

ACKNOWLEDGEMENTS

To my beautiful sister, thank you so much for sticking by my side through this whole process. I couldn't have done it without you. You're always the person I can count on to always be there for me and support me no matter what I do. You're my best friend, my little sister, and my motivation for life most times. Thank you for always bringing out the magic in life and making my dark nights always so much brighter. You are the sunshine in my life and I am so thankful to call you my sister. Thank you for encouraging me to always follow my dreams. I can only hope that everyone knows someone as great as you.

    Thank you to my best friends for also encouraging me to always follow my dreams. You guys showed me that family doesn't always have to be by blood. You are truly my found family and I wouldn't have it any other way. I love you guys with all my heart.

To my parents, thank you for always telling me I could do whatever I want in life as long as I set my mind to it. Especially the last few years, you have encouraged me to go for what I want and to never settle. Thank you.

To my cat, thank you so much for standing on my computer when I was trying to write. If it wasn't for you I would've had this done months earlier. <3

To my boyfriend, thank you for showing me what true love looks like. It is not always like it is in the books and movies, but what we have is better. You are my best friend and I can't imagine going through life with anyone but you. You have taught me so much and it has been so fun to grow up with you all these years and mature into who are today, *together*. I never imagined getting along with someone so well at such a young age and I am lucky to have found you.

To all that amazing people who helped out with this book THANK YOU! Ozge Demir, I could go on for pages and pages thanking you for the amazing cover illustration. Your talent and passion for art is made so clear through your work. Thank you a million times for capturing my vision and making the cover of my dreams. You made something truly magical and I will forever be grateful. I looked for the right artist for days and as soon as you sent me that initial sketch, I knew that you were the one for this project. Anna Dolidze, thank you for the beautiful map illustration. I am so grateful that I get to have your beautiful art work represent my story. You took my horrible sketch of ideas and turned it into something I am so proud of. To Kaylee Pryble and Aaliyah Hernandez for editing my manuscript. You both helped to make this a beautiful piece to read. To my beta readers Molli O'neil and Aaliyah Hernandez, thank you for all your hard work to make my story better and reading when the story wasn't so polished. I couldn't have done it with out you both.

Most of all, thank you to *you*. To the readers who took a chance on me and decided to pick up my book. You make everything worthwhile. Here's to many more stories and adventures that we will have together.

-Nareena Rhoman

Printed in Great Britain
by Amazon